Wilkes the Wizard
and the S.P.A.M.

By the same author

Wilkes the Wizard

JACKIE WEBB

Wilkes the Wizard and the S.P.A.M.

Illustrated by Steve Smallman

GRAFTON BOOKS

A Division of the Collins Publishing Group

LONDON GLASGOW
TORONTO SYDNEY AUCKLAND

Grafton Books
A Division of the Collins Publishing Group
8 Grafton Street, London W1X 3LA

Published by Grafton Books 1986

British Library Cataloguing in Publication Data
Webb, Jackie
   Wilkes the wizard and the S.P.A.M.
   I. Title   II. Smallman, Steve
   823′.914[J]   PZ7

ISBN 0 246 12916 6

Printed in Great Britain by Billing & Sons Ltd, Worcester

Contents

1

Starting with a lot of old rubbish

'No!' growled the Gram Tam of Diddlesdorf. 'No, I won't! I'm not signing any state papers, or anything, until you give me my boots back.'

'Don't be absurd, Percival,' barked the Gram Duchess. 'Come along – the Prime Minister needs your signature. She hasn't got all day.'

'And I haven't got my boots. . .'

'I should think not! Polishing your boots with a clean tea-towel! Whoever *heard* of such a thing? Now stop sulking and sign those papers at once.' And off marched the Duchess, pearls rattling, in search of a scullery maid to put the tea-towel into the washing machine.

'They're only *little* papers, sire,' coaxed the Prime Minister. 'You'll hardly notice them.'

But the Gram Tam was peering crossly out of the window through paper binoculars, cunningly made of two rolled-up documents.

'They're all about your favourite project, sire!'

No answer.

'Don't you want to know what it is?'

Still no answer.

'They're to authorize a new municipal rubbish tip!'

'Don't care.'

'Oh, but sire!' The little old lady twinkled at him through her small gold-rimmed spectacles. 'You *want* a new rubbish tip – you *know* you do.'

'I don't! I don't want any rubbishy old tip. I want my walking boots and I want to polish them up to go . . . you know – walking . . . and survey my whatsit! Survey my realm! That's what I want. And now my wife's gone off with my boots, and put my cleaning cloth in the washing machine, and. . . !' And off he stomped. Then he changed his mind, and stomped back again. 'And you can stuff your papers in the . . . in the . . . raspberry jam! See if I care!'

Well, I don't know about you, but if I were Prime Minister of Diddlesdorf, I'd give up.

Not Peony Moondrop. She hurried back to her little office, sat down, put up her feet, and thought. 'Heigh-ho!' she said to herself. 'Two heads are better than one – as the Alien said to the spaceman.' So she phoned her friend the Wizard, asking him to come and give her a hand (or rather, a head, if you follow my meaning).

'I'm having a spot of bother with His Exigency,' she said. 'I think we need a brainstorming session.'

And that was how it was that the Prime Minister and the Wizard spent the afternoon shut up in the broom cupboard. The little old lady stood on her head and juggled with her feet, while the Wizard, in his great black robe all stitched with mystic symbols, sat with *his* feet in the waste-paper basket, doodling the insides of atoms on the blotting paper. And they thought . . . and thought . . . and thought. . .

What do you mean – this story isn't making sense? Of *course* it is!

Peony Moondrop (now Prime Minister of Diddlesdorf) used to be an acrobat in the circus.

The Prime Minister's office (now an office) used to be a broom cupboard.

And Mr Bob Wilkes (now Wizard to the Gram Tam of Diddlesdorf) used to be a sub-atomic particle physicist. Well, poor soul, he couldn't help it.

So naturally, the Wizard tended to draw sub-atomic particles while he was thinking up spells – and the Prime Minister found that her head was clearer if she stood on it. And the office, unfortunately, hadn't grown an inch since it was a broom cupboard. So, if you had two people in it at once, one of them had to put his feet in the waste-paper basket. Right?

And the Gram Tam?

Well, he always was a problem. It wasn't that he was a difficult chap. No, he was nice enough – affable, didn't scold his children (often), played a decent game of Space Invaders. He even made a reasonable job of ruling Diddlesdorf, so long as he did as his wife told him.

The problem was that, two years ago, he had had an Idea. Just the one of it – he wasn't prone to lots of them – but it had been very troublesome ever since.

The Gram Tam's Idea was very simple: what Diddlesdorf needed was less policy, and more Magic. Magic, excitement, adventure – that sort of thing. Diddlesdorf might be very small, but it would be *different*. So he found himself a Wizard – well, he found Mr Wilkes, anyway.

Of course, Mr Wilkes couldn't actually do *magic*. He couldn't have made so much as a magic button. He wasn't a *real* Wizard. But, given an average-looking lunatic with an orange beard and silly clothes, who can do physics and electronics – who's to know the difference?

Especially when he invented the Hoverrug! Everybody loved the Hoverrug. Who could resist a fluffy flying carpet that hovered a few feet off the ground? When crowds of tourists came flocking into Diddlesdorf, paying good money to have a go on one, even the Gram Duchess began to think a Wizard might have his uses!

But, oh dear, you know how it is. Somebody has a really stunning new idea, something earth-shattering, something to take the world by the ears and make its toes curl – and then the sensible ideas latch on. Before you know where you are, everything's trundling along in the boring old normal way.

Mr Wilkes did his best. He made the Gram Tam a magic bow-tie, magic golf-ball (couldn't get lost), magic tea-stirrer, a funny magic box for falling off shelves – fell off any shelf you put it on – oh, magic bits and bobs of all sorts. Hours of fun they were too. But whenever he had a real brilliancy – something really big, like a huge fountain for Mulberry Square that turned water into fizzy lemonade – sensible objections came plodding in and ruined everything. Too expensive, said Secretary Fizzell; no room for it, said the Duchess; it would upset such-and-such a committee, or you can't do it without so-and-so's permission. And so on, and so on. . .

No wonder the Gram Tam was beginning to get bored! No wonder he wanted his walking boots when everybody knew he never walked further than the chip shop. Things were looking dangerous. Somebody would have to *do* something, quickly, before His Exigency started having Ideas again!

Luckily, no such thing had happened yet. The Gram Tam that afternoon was sitting harmlessly in his study, sorting his Royal Collection. Not porcelain, or silver, or Old Masters. No – Bingo cards.

The Gram Tam had the very finest collection of unused bingo cards in the known universe. He'd saved them from every newspaper under the Sun – except for the odd one or two that don't have them. Now he was sorting them, according to a system devised by his own royal person, into various brown paper bags.

'What are you going to do with them, sire?' asked P.M., who'd sidled into his study with the state papers hidden in her skirt.

'Er, send them to Brown – er, Blue . . . Blue Peter. Blue Peter! Got a fine collection here, you know. Some here three years old!'

'How very nice, sire. Do Blue Peter actually *want* old bingo cards, sire?'

'Bound to. One of these days. . .' And the Gram Tam carefully sorted a bright green bingo card into a paper bag. 'I'm not doing it, you know.'

P.M. twinkled sweetly over her glasses. 'Not doing what, sire?'

'Signing those thingummies. Those papers. Not doing it. . .'

'Of course not, sire! Wouldn't dream of asking such a thing. On the other hand, the Wizard has just had a fantastic idea – his best invention yet! Oh, Your Exigency, you're going to be thrilled to bits. He's working on it now.'

'Oh, er . . . really? What is it, this, er. . . ?'

'Well naturally, we can't tell you that until we've got a little signature – here – and here.'

It was quite easy. The Gram Tam huffed, and snorted, and grumbled, and signed the papers. Then P.M. whispered something in his ear, and skipped away before the papers could get unsigned again.

'Oh, er . . . P.M.,' called the Gram Tam before she closed the door. 'What were those, er. . . ? Those things I just signed?'

'About the rubbish tip, sire. *Terribly* important. . .'

'Tip? Good Lord, why didn't you *tell* me? Should have been done months ago! Old one's bursting at the, er . . . bursting at the . . . whatsits.'

'Seams, sire.'

'Seems what?'

P.M. scurried out to look for a nip of gin, by way of de-Gramtamination.

Instead of that, she got Fizzell, the Gram Tam's Private Secretary, looking particularly efficient.

'Ah, Prime Minister,' he said, frowning at his large efficient clipboard file. 'We need His Exigency's signature on these papers relating to the Municipal Refuse Facility.'

'You mean the Tip?'

'The Refuse Facility – that's correct. As a matter of urgency.'

'But I've just got him to sign *these* papers about the Tip!'

'New proposals, new proposals. A matter of *absolute* urgency. . .'

P.M. would have been tearing her hair out – except that she'd done it up in such a neat little bun, it seemed a pity to disturb it.

No peace for a Prime Minister. No sooner had she escaped the dreaded Fizzell than she almost bumped into somebody's knees on the stairs. Way above the knees was the very grand and lofty personage of the Duke of Potshotts. He took out a monocle, and peered down at her.

'Ah, Prime Minister!' he said. 'Just the chap I was looking for. Got a bit of a shock this morning.'

'A shock, your Grace?'

'Nasty shock. Chappie came round from the Municipal Refuse Department. Wanted to size up my safari park for a waste tip!'

'Your safari park? For the waste tip. . . .' Suddenly, Fizzell's 'new proposals' leapt to P.M.'s mind: she put her hand to her mouth in horror.

'Can't have it, you know. Won't tolerate it. Defend my safari park to the death, you know.'

Can you imagine it? The Duke of Potshotts defending his safari park to the death against the Municipal Refuse Department! An idea too shocking to contemplate. P.M. thought she had better hurry the Duke along to the Gram Tam at once and sort things out.

They were nearly too late. His Exigency was already putting his fountain pen into his 'Mr Men' pencil-case, and Secretary Fizzell, clutching his signed papers, was hurrying out of the door. The Duke of Potshotts glared at him down the full grandeur of a very long nose. Fizzell backed into the study again.

'Out of the question. Utterly out of the question!' declared the Duke.

'What's that, your Grace?' Fizzell had a silly smile in the middle of his fat face, like a pie funnel in the middle of a big round pastry crust.

'Do you know, Your Exigency,' said the Duke, turning to the Gram Tam (who was still trying to do up the zip on his pencil-case). 'Do you know what's *in* those documents you've just signed?'

'Er, same as before. Um, same as P.M.'s . . . er, waste paper – er, rubbish . . . er, rubbish tip.'

'Have you read the thing, sire?'

'Well, um . . . er. . .'

'Thought not. Well, this fellow,' and the Duke stared witheringly at Fizzell. 'This fellow is proposing to put a rubbish tip in my safari park! Dash it all, sire, it's out of the question!'

'Good heavens, Fizzell,' said the Gram Tam. 'It's the Duke's question. Er . . . safari park. Out of the question.'

'Hardly a park, sire,' simpered Fizzell. 'More of a paddock, I'd call it.'

'It's a safari park!' declared the Duke.

'Well, a safari paddock, perhaps. It's just a field with a few trees. . .'

'. . . a safari park!! It's got a lion in it!'

'Good Lord – a lion, y'know, Fizzell,' said the Gram Tam helpfully. 'We can't go putting municipal rubbish in a safari paddock with a lion! It might, er . . . it might, um . . . it might. . .'

Well, of course, it might.

But Fizzell was not to be put off by the odd lion. 'Now look, sire – it's absolutely essential that we have a new refuse facility. Urgently! The old one's on the point of falling down.'

'Falling down, you know,' explained the Gram Tam to the Duke.

'And we can't site the new facility up the mountain. . .'

'Fall off, you know,' explained the Gram Tam to the Duke.

'. . . nowhere else in Diddlesdorf we could use. There is no alternative!'

'No alternative!' explained the Gram Tam.

The Duke was turning a very grand shade of purple. 'This is monstrous! Where's my lion going to go?!'

'Build it a kennel,' suggested Fizzell.

'Dash it all, man – you don't put lions in kennels. Besides, you can't go taking over a fellow's safari padd . . . safari park without so much as a by-your-leave!' The Duke turned to P.M., who had been sitting quietly in a corner making notes in a little book. 'It's against the law, what?'

P.M. put her head on one side to think, like a bird listening for a worm. 'Well, Duke,' she said, looking at Fizzell out of the corner of her eye. 'We should have to pay you an awful lot of money for it. . .'

'Of course,' – Fizzell was suddenly looking uncomfortable – 'Of course, this was only an *idea*.

Nothing definite. We might not use the Duke's
safari paddock after all.'

'Of course, we might not use it, you know,' said
the Gram Tam, retrieving a halfpenny from down
the back of the sofa, and putting it in his pocket.
'Especially if, er . . . if it costs money, you know.'

'But it's still urgent!' said Fizzell. 'It's of vital
importance, sire, this refuse facility.'

'Ah! Vital, er. . .' The Gram Tam was poking
down the back of the sofa with a pencil, bringing up
pieces of fluff. 'Vital. . .'

'If the Duke's paddock isn't available, we'll just
have to go to the Wizard, sire. Make him earn his
keep! Get him to make us a magic rubbish dump!'

'Got it!' exclaimed the Gram Tam triumphantly.

Everyone looked. Everyone looked quite hopeful.

'Found the boot polish!' announced the Gram Tam happily, pulling a small brown tin out of the sofa. '*Now* I can polish my boots.'

2

How the Gram Tam went to see the Devil and met somebody else instead

It was a Monday morning, and a bright yellow dressing gown was wandering around the Palace corridors with the Gram Tam in it. He looked lost.

'What are you doing, Percival?' The Duchess, already washed and dressed, was going around like a mine-sweeper – looking for trouble and putting an end to it. 'Hurry up and get washed!'

'I'm *trying* to hurry up. I can't find a blasted bathroom.'

The Palace, a large semi-detached, had five bathrooms to choose from. On the other hand, the Gram Tam had five daughters.

'Wait here,' said the Duchess, 'until Wanda comes out of the pink-and-green bathroom.'

'But I'm in a hurry! I'm going out. . .'

'Do as you're told.'

So the Gram Tam had to fume and fret in the corridor until his eldest-daughter-but-one came out of the pink-and-green bathroom.

When he finally appeared at the breakfast table he announced that he wasn't having any.

'And where,' enquired the Duchess, 'do you think you're going?'

'Not telling you!' he grumped. 'I've found the boot-polish; I've abolished my poots, and I'm . . . I'm . . . going out! And what are you two laughing at?' He glared at his two youngest daughters.

'Just be quite sure that you're back by two,' said

the Duchess. 'Remember what day it is.'

'Of course I know what day it is. It's Tu -We -n - Thur . . . It's in the *calendar*!'

'It's Monday. The day you greet the new tourists and welcome them to Diddlesdorf.'

'Oh . . . FIDDLESTICKS!'

'Percival, behave yourself. *You* wanted the tourists in the first place. You wanted to advertise Diddlesdorf as the Land of the Magic Carpet. Now the least you can do is to wave at the holiday-makers and tell them to enjoy themselves.'

'Hmph!' The Gram Tam clumped off in his walk-ing boots. 'Enjoy themselves!' he mumbled. 'They're not going to enjoy anybody *else*, are they?'

'You ever seen the Wizard's Workshop?' Freddi, the punk footman peered into the cupboard under the stairs, his mauve hairdo standing stiffly upright as though he'd just seen a lot of purple ghosts. 'Eh? Rick?'

Rick crawled out cobwebbed, clutching the gar-den chair he'd been sent in for. 'Yer what?'

'Ever seen inside the Wizard's Workshop?'

'Cor!' Rick wiped his dirty hands on his foot-man's tee-shirt, and shook his head.

'Well here's your chance, then. We gotta go and fetch a magic table.'

I dare say you're familiar with a Wizard's Work-shop? You can imagine dusty piles of ancient tomes, marked with runes and mystic symbols? Cauldrons full of evil green liquids, retorts giving off strange purple vapours, the orreries hung with spiders' webs, vile dried fungi, bats' wings, snake-

20

skins, toads preserved in sinister jars, newts'-eyes, dead men's fingernails – that sort of thing?

Well, I don't know: what rubbish have you been reading?

Mr Wilkes had arranged his Workshop just as he liked it. He had a computer, with VDU and disc-drive, naturally, and a printer, two shelves of software, plus four of books (mostly on 'Advanced Machine Code' and stuff like that). Further along the bench was an oscilloscope, power-supply, volt-meter, soldering iron, stacks of printed circuit-boards, and four cabinets with hundreds of little drawers full of electronic components. Not a pick-led toad in sight.

'Cor!' said Rick, gazing around with his mouth open. 'Where's this table then?'

'You're leaning on it,' said the Wizard with a grin.

The two footmen peered at the table: it looked quite spectacularly boring. A plain old kitchen table – formica top, and two drawers underneath; you know the sort of thing.

'What's it do?'

Mr Wilkes took a handful of paperclips, a tea-spoon and a drawing pin, and put them on the table. He rummaged in his pockets, added a little heap of coins and a comb. Then he sauntered up the other end of the Workshop and seemed to be staring out of the window.

'Uh?' said Rick.

Suddenly, they went berserk. (The oddments, I mean, not the footmen.) The comb and the tea-spoon skated around like mad things; pins and paperclips slithered into tangled heaps; the pile of

coins lurched drunkenly from side to side, tottered, and collapsed. . .

Rick was baffled. Nobody had touched them. The table never moved a millimetre. What on earth had got into them? The Wizard grinned into his beard.

Freddi was poking about underneath, pulling out the drawers. . . .

'Got it!' he crowed. There in the drawers were four electro-magnets. 'Must have some kind of remote control, somewhere. What yer got, then? One off a telly?'

Mr Wilkes burst out laughing, and owned up. He'd got one in his pocket. 'Freddi, you should have been a Wizard!'

Now, I have a suggestion to make. If it's a nice, simple, straightforward story you want, one where nothing goes haywire, why not put this book down and read something else?

Nothing was ever straightforward in Diddlesdorf.

This table, for instance – all they had to do was to take it to the Gram Tam in his study. Well. . .

For a start, the Gram Tam wasn't in; he was out in his walking boots. And he'd locked his study and taken the key. So they went to look for the spare keys, which were hidden safely away, as everybody knew, in the silver teapot.

Except that they weren't.

'Oh,' said a maid, 'I moved 'em, when I was cleaning the silver. I put 'em in with those old fish-knives.'

And where were the fish-knives? Somebody had sold them to an antique dealer. And the antique dealer? He'd sold them to a tourist. And the tourist? He'd flown back to Texas that very morning, with the fish-knives – and half the keys to the Palace of Diddlesdorf.

'Well,' said Rick, 'That's triffic, innit?'

So they put the magic table in the bathroom, until the Gram Tam came back. But that, I'm warning you, was not the end of the matter.

The Gram Tam, meanwhile, was walking backwards. Well, having got his walking boots on, he thought he'd better do *something*.

So he decided to try something he'd had in mind for years. Halfway up Diddlesdorf's mountain, there was a hole in the ground – a long narrow chasm. You couldn't see far down; it was too dark. But way down below were huge caves, so people

23

said. They called it the Devil's Kitchen. If you walked round it seven times backwards, so the story ran, you'd hear the Devil frying his pancakes.

Well, thought the Gram Tam, it was worth a try. So here he was, puffing like a walrus, on his third lap. He'd just got to the awkward, knobbly bit, where the grass grew in tussocks, when – WHUMP!

'Ah! . . . er . . . er . . . ha-ha! . . . er.' said the Gram Tam.

'Well, hullo there!' said a big American voice. And the man he'd bumped into shook his hand warmly, several times, as though he might pump some sense out of him.

'I was . . . er . . . just walking backwards. . .'

'*Right*!' agreed the man enthusiastically, as if this was an activity that everyone should approve of. 'I'm Jay G. Schickenburger.'

'Ah – er, right!' said the Gram Tam. 'I'm the, er, Gram Tam. Of, er, Diddlesdorf.'

'Right!' agreed Mr Schickenburger. He was a short man, with a check jacket, and a small amount of hair, carefully arranged to make it go further. 'Well,' he bellowed, 'Am I glad to meet *you*, sir! The Gram Tam! I understand you own this little – er-hem, this great little country?'

'Well, er . . . hereditary ruler, you know.'

Mr Schickenburger seemed overjoyed at this, and so they got talking – about ruling Diddlesdorf, and making money, and Diddlesdorf's natural advantages, and tourists, and making money, and making money, and so on. At least, Jay G. Schickenburger talked about those things, and the Gram Tam nodded sagely and looked as though he'd have

said the same, of course. Then Mr Schickenburger asked him something about the Gross National Product.

'Er, gross, um. . . Would you like a go on my Hoverrug?' he said.

'Wow-ee!' said Mr Schickenburger. 'One of *the* famous Diddlesdorf Flying Carpets? Wouldn't I just! Y'know, I never flew a magic carpet before. . .'

The Gram Tam waved his hand nonchalently, and clumped down the hill in his boots. 'Just down here,' he said. 'Parked it behind that rock.'

He hadn't. It was the wrong rock. So they tried the other path, and it wasn't that one either. So they trudged back up to the Devil's Kitchen and started again, and found it behind a completely different rock. It sat there looking very like a cheap fluffy pink bedroom rug with seatbelts.

'Just a little runaround my Wizard made for me, you know. Er, jump on. Show you round the country, if you like.'

So the Gram Tam strapped himself on, and Mr Schickenburger perched precariously on the back, hanging on to the Gram Tam's waist. Or at any rate, he hung on to that area of the Gram Tam where you would normally expect to find a waist. The Gram Tam switched on.

The Hoverrug's engines spluttered, moaned and heaved. Up it came at the back, like a shocking pink pancake trying to flip over – and flump! – down it went again.

'Carrying a spot more weight than, um, usual,' explained the Gram Tam.

'Right!' agreed Mr Schickenburger anxiously.

The Hoverrug tried again, with a will. This time it hauled itself up into the air – several inches above the ground. Then it proceeded, huffing and chugging, down the mountainside and into the town. 'Wow-ee!' said Mr Schickenburger. He was bowled over by everything – the magic rugs, the Gram Tam, the Gram Tam's splendid hat, Diddlesdorf, the pretty views, and all the people wearing cheerful orange badges. After all, Mr Schickenburger wasn't to know what the badges actually said. ('WHAT A DUMP!' they protested, campaigning for a new rubbish tip.) Nor was he to know that the

26

pretty views were mostly of next-door countries, or that the Gram Tam's splendiferous hat originally came from a jumble sale. So what? Everything looked marvellous, and what was more to the point (in Mr Schickenburger's opinion), everything he saw had 'tourist potential'.

'Wow! – this sure has tourist potential!' exclaimed Mr Schickenburger at every corner.

'Er, hello dear,' called the Gram Tam, when they finally reached the Palace. 'Mr Chickenburger thinks we've got tourist potential! Er . . . hello!'

But the Gram Duchess wasn't in her sitting-room after all.

So the Gram Tam went to look in the dining-room, with Mr Jay G. Schickenburger hurrying along behind. 'Er, hello – er, this is Mr Chickenburger from Texas, and . . . er. . .'

But the Duchess wasn't in the dining-room either.

'Try the kitchen,' said the Gram Tam to the puzzled Mr Schickenburger. 'Hello! Muriel! Mr Kitchenburger from, er . . . oh . . .'

The Duchess wasn't in the kitchen, either. Naturally, she'd gone along to the antique-shop to deal with the matter of the escaped fish-knives.

So the Gram Tam was left to his own devices. 'Ah, er . . . come along to my study and we'll, um, sign that whatsit. That document. Right away, eh? Never put off till the present what you can . . . er, can do tomorrow, I always say. Er, something like that.'

Mr Schickenburger gave the Gram Tam a big Texan slap on the back, and congratulated him heartily on his wise decision. 'All I need is your sig-

27

nature on that little old dotted line, right away!'

'I, er, I usually just put "Percival G.T." . . . um. . .'

Mr Schickenburger assured His Exigency that that would do fine, just *absolutely* fine.

The only problem was, they couldn't seem to get into the study. The Gram Tam pulled the door, pushed the door, rattled the door. . .

'I'd say that door's locked, at this moment in time,' observed Mr Jay G. Schickenburger.

'Er, can't get in,' said the Gram Tam.

His Exigency seemed to think that this was a good reason for dithering. But Mr Schickenburger didn't want to delay a moment. 'Any place will do. How about next door?'

'In here? Er . . . bathroom. No desk. My Wizard, you know, my Wizard's making me a magic table! Wish we'd got it here now, eh? Oops! What, er. . . ?'

The Gram Tam had just backed into his magic table.

'Er . . . Ha! Magic table! Comes when I call, you see. "Wish I had my magic table" – and WHOOSH!, magic table, d'you see? Good, eh?'

Mr Schickenburger was breathless with enthusiasm. 'Fantastic! How *about* that? Turns up at just the perfect moment – now if you'll just sign this document here, where I've put a cross. . .'

So the Gram Tam, positively glowing with his own brilliance, signed the document.

'Ah, Percival, there you are!' The Duchess was coming in at the front door, just as the Gram Tam was about to let Mr Schickenburger out of it.

'Oh, er . . . Hello, er . . . This is my wife, the, er, Gram Duchess. This is Mr Shillingburger, and he's from Texas, and he's um . . . um. . .'

'Jay G. Schickenburger, ma'am. Am I glad to meet you!'

'Oh good,' said the Duchess. 'How very convenient. From Texas – now, a gentleman from Texas has just gone home with our fish-knives, and all the spare keys to the Palace. Perhaps you'd be good enough to pop in on your way home, Mr Shippingburger .'

'Well now, ma'am. . .'

'Simply ask him to return the entire box, at once, please. It's a Mr Hank Woolman – maybe you know him? Here's the address: Lubbock, Texas.'

Mr Schickenburger shook his head. Patiently he explained to the Duchess that Texas was a very big place, that he lived in Houston, that Lubbock was five or six hundred miles away, that he'd never been there, never expected to, and had never heard of Mr Woolman.

'Oh,' said the Duchess, disappointed. 'So you don't think you'll be passing?'

'No, ma'am.'

Nevertheless, the Duchess got over it, and politely asked Mr Schickenburger to lunch.

The Gram Tam seemed awfully excited about something. 'Guess what!' he whispered loudly to the Duchess. 'Guess what!'

The Duchess told him to behave himself and be quiet while she introduced their guest to the five daughters. Winifred, Wanda, Wisteria, Wilhelmina and Wendy each had to shake hands and say – 'How do you do, Mr Schickenburger,' which they did quite well until it came to Wendy, who got the giggles, was told off, and had to do it all over again.

Then they all sat down to Spaghetti Bolognaise, while the Gram Tam whispered, 'Guess what! Guess what?'

'Percival!' scolded the Duchess, keeping on her smile – the best starched one that she used when they had guests. 'Stop whispering and watch your spaghetti.'

The Gram Tam watched his spaghetti. He watched it hard as it uncoiled itself from his fork and slithered down his waistcoat. He watched it slide gracefully down his trousers and on to the carpet. 'I, er . . . I watched,' he said.

The Gram Duchess took a deep breath and aimed her smile fiercely at the guest. 'Well, Mr Schickenburger, how do you like Diddlesdorf?'

'Absolutely delighted with it!' said Mr Schickenburger.

'Oh, really?'

'Yes ma'am – I don't think I ever made a better deal!'

'Oh, real. . .' It took a moment or two to sink in. '*What* did I hear you say? A deal! On *Diddlesdorf*?'

'Not Diddlesdorf, ma'am. Not any longer.' Mr Schickenburger thrust a large American smile right across the table. 'Magicland! That's right – better than Disneyland. . .'

'*Magicland!*'

'Right, ma'am. I have the little old document right here – His Exigency signed it this morning. This place is gonna be THE most phenomenal theme park in the little old WORLD!'

There was a frozen silence.

'Percival. . .' The Duchess, slowly rising from her chair, fixed on the Gram Tam a dragon stare of dreadful wrath. 'What have you to say about this?'

'Um . . . um – You, er . . . you've got spaghetti caught in your necklace. .'

3

All to do with small print

'Have you heard?' – the news slipped out of the dining-room with the dirty dinner-plates, and was all round the Palace in two shakes of a dishcloth. The Palace canteen was in uproar.

'He hasn't!'

'He has!'

'He's swapped the lot of us for Seven Dwarfs!'

'No, you wally – not swapped. He's sold Diddles-dorf. . .'

'. . . to an American!'

'. . . for millions of dollars!'

''E ain't sellin' me. I ain't goin'!'

'. . . we're all going to get rich – for dressing up as Seven Dwarfs, so's the tourists can come and look. . .'

'But I'm too big for a dwarf. . .'

'QUIET!' came a familiar bellow, like a cross between a very high trombone and a singing donkey. 'Quiet, please!' It was the Gram Duchess at the canteen door. 'We have a crisis.'

'Not *another* one!' groaned somebody at the back.

'We had a crisis last week,' piped up a scullery maid. 'Can't we have a barn dance this time?'

The Duchess clamped her mouth into a short, tight line and looked explosive. Everyone shushed the hecklers. 'We have a crisis,' the Duchess went on. 'All leave will therefore be cancelled . . .'

'Oh, *no*!'

'. . . all leave will be cancelled until further

notice. Furthermore, I want to make it perfectly clear that whatever you may have heard is *utter* nonsense. Diddlesdorf is *not* being sold to a Texas millionaire; it is *not* being packed up and sent to America; it is *not* being turned into a holiday camp for pixies. All these rumours must stop forthwith!'

'Fourth what?' Murmurs sprang up, and slunk away again when the Duchess looked at them.

'Is this quite clear to everybody? The Gram Tam will go on being in charge of Diddlesdorf – and I shall go on being in charge of the Gram Tam. Exactly as before. Now you can all eat your pudding, and say no more about it.'

And having put that straight, the Duchess made a triumphant return to the royal dining-room to put Mr Schickenburger straight too. Unfortunately, there was a snag.

'Where's Mr Schickenburger?'

'Oh, he's er . . . gone,' said the Gram Tam.

'Gone? What do you mean – gone?'

'Well, er . . . you know, um . . . not come. Sort of, walked out.'

'You let him go!' the Duchess screeched like chalk on a blackboard. '*You* were supposed to keep him talking while I went to speak to the servants!'

'Well, I er, ran out of things to say.'

The Duchess closed her eyes in despair. Then, remembering that time was short, she opened them again, and sent the girls to their rooms. All except Winifred, who was the eldest daughter and very sensible.

'Winifred,' ordered the Duchess, 'Run after Mr Schickenburger, and bring him back here.'

But Winifred had an even more sensible idea.

34

She phoned the taxi company. 'Has one of your taxis picked up an American from our Palace?' she asked.

'Yes,' they said.

'Well, call the taxi-driver on your radio, and tell him to turn straight round and bring him back. My mother wants to speak to him.' And she put the phone down before they could argue.

The Duchess meanwhile was hard at work extracting information from the Gram Tam. 'Yes, but Percival, what did the small print say?'

'Small print, er. . .' The Gram Tam looked around vaguely.

'In the *document*, Percival. What did the small print say?'

'Oh, er, document. Didn't read it. But just think, Muriel – Magicland! Magic, Mystery, Adventure, all that. . .'

'So who is going to pay?'

'What?'

'Who is paying for all this? This Mystery, Adventure, Magic – who's paying for them? Mr Schickenburger?'

'Oh, er . . . Yes, I suppose, er – well. . .'

'Is he or isn't he? What did you *agree*?'

'Um, well . . . er. . . He's not just a *man*, you know, Mr Chickenburger. More of a company. He's incorporated! Said so on the top – the, er, document.'

'You mean, he represents a tour company, or an airline, perhaps?'

'Um, yes. Well, probably. Er, holidays. . . Lots of rich American tourists, he said, all coming to see Magicland! Plenty of knights in armour, we want, and enchanted castles, and, er, thingies – you know, ogres, and stuff like that. Oh, and damsons. . .'

'*Damsels*.'

'That's the stuff, um. . . They're the plums, aren't they?'

Talking of plums, the Duchess was looking a bit red and mushy herself. 'I cannot make you see *sense*,' she cried. 'You've got a Wizard. You've got flying carpets everywhere. You've got all kinds of ridiculous magical novelties. Why this? Why turn the entire country into a tasteless version of Grimms' Fairy Tales?!'

'Well – fun, you know.'

'Fun!' shrieked the Duchess. 'Fun! Making me into some kind of second-hand Fairy Queen! At my time of life! It's not *proper*.'

'Er, tell you what,' said the Gram Tam, seeing the Duchess's desperation-level rising fast, 'I'll just go and watch my "Dr Who" video – and then I'll, er, think of something. How about that?'

Fortunately, at that point, a pot of tea poked its spout round the door. It was followed shortly by Peony Moondrop. 'A cup of tea – always the best thing in a crisis, ma'am,' she said. 'And then it will be time for His Exigency to go and greet the new tourists.'

'Oh, goodness – it's Monday!' exclaimed the Duchess. 'They'll all be waiting in Mulberry Square. You'd better go at once, Percival.'

'Ah, yes. Er, tourists. . . Er, "Dr Who", you know – my video – Oh, never mind. Tourists, yes. Right. Ex-term-in-ate! Ex-term-in-ate!' And the Gram Tam went out to greet the tourists, one arm

held stiffly in front of him like a sink-plunger. 'Ex -
term-in-ate!'

The Duchess gratefully took a cup of tea and an
aspirin. 'I'm at my wit's end,' she complained.
'Goodness knows, I do *try* to keep a check on what's
happening. But it's like trying to guess the weight of
the cake, in the pitch dark, in the middle of a thun-
derstorm, while the cake keeps leaping up and
walking away!'

P.M. was optimistic. Mr Schickenburger would
be arriving back in a minute or two. Then they
could look at the document for themselves, and sort
everything out. 'You see!' she said. 'It'll only take
five minutes.'

Well, it didn't.

Five, ten, fifteen minutes they waited – no sign of
a taxi, no Mr Schickenburger, no document. They
phoned the taxi company a second time. Winifred
was sent out to watch for anyone arriving at the
Palace.

Ten minutes later he turned up. No – not Mr
Schickenburger. The Gram Tam.

'Oh NO!' they cried.

What had happened? Well, the Gram Tam had
gone out, taking his umbrella. (No, it wasn't raining, but the Gram Tam worried about falling ice-
creams from passing aeroplanes). Anyway, he had
just walked a few yards down the street, when who
should he see but Mr Chickenburger (I do beg his
pardon: *Schickenburger*) looking bewildered in a
taxi. Naturally, the Gram Tam waved. In fact he
waved his umbrella vigorously. Whereupon the
taxi-driver, assuming His Exigency to be hailing the
taxi, stopped at once and opened the door for him.

Now the Gram Tam hadn't wanted a taxi at all. But seeing it standing there, with the door open for him, he naturally got in. And then, as the taxi-driver seemed to be waiting for him to say something, he said 'Mulberry Square'.

So Mulberry Square it was. By this time Mr Schickenburger was peering anxiously at his watch. 'Where the blazes are we going *now*? I'm gonna miss that plane. . .'

Well, to cut a long story short, they ended up at the airport, where Mr Schickenburger leapt out in a hurry – and forgot the document. By that time, the Gram Tam had forgotten where he was going, and asked to be dropped off at the Palace.

Had he brought the document?

'The what?'

'The document! Have you got it!'

'No. Left it in the taxi.'

There was a short break for gnashing of teeth, tearing of hair, and so forth.

Then the Duchess demanded action. The document *must* be found. No-one knew what was going on until they'd read the document: it must be found *at once*. Winifred was sent to phone the poor taxi-company yet again. Secretary Fizzell was sent for and didn't come; the Steward was sent to the Police; two housemaids were sent to ask at the bus station, and the footmen were sent out on to the streets of Diddlesdorf to stop and search any taxi they could find.

And the Gram Tam? He was sent back to Mulberry Square. The tourists had probably given up and gone home by now, but still. . . What else could you do with him?

'What *can* you do with him?' complained the Duchess, as P.M. dialled the Wizard's phone number. 'This is absolutely the last straw. This frightful row over the new rubbish tip, the traffic wardens demanding a pay rise, the new bedroom carpet clashing with the curtains – and now this! P.M., I begin to feel that Providence is deliberately trying to make me lose my temper. Where's Fizzell? I called him ten minutes ago.'

'It's Monday, ma'am,' said P.M., still waiting for a reply from the Wizard. 'Fizzell's half-day.'

'There you are! What did I tell you? A constitutional crisis on our hands, and our Private Secretary's away on his half-day! If disasters go on happening at this rate, I shall have no alternative but to use a swear word.'

'Oh, I'm sure it won't come to that, ma'am. Dash it! – where the blazes has this Wizard got to?' P.M. slammed the phone down – and burst into giggles. 'Oh dear!'

So they couldn't find the Wizard anywhere, but they found General Storr without too much trouble. In fact, they found him tapping on the sitting-room window and making funny faces.

'What's up?' asked P.M., opening the window.

'Can't make anybody hear,' complained the General. 'Front doorbell's not working.'

'That's *all* we need!' said the Duchess.

They let him in.

'Absolutely out of the question, ma'am,' said the General firmly.

'Of course it is,' said the Duchess. 'What is? Who says so?'

'The army, ma'am. They've been hearing this

rumour, and they're not happy. They're a professional army, and they don't want to be turned into a bunch of tin-pot pantomime soldiers just to amuse a lot of lolly-licking, camera-clicking foreigners!' The General took a deep breath, and looked at his notes. 'I think I got that right.'

'Don't be silly, General,' said the Duchess. 'It's just a foolish rumour. Now you go straight back and tell your soldiers to behave themselves.'

But the General was adamant. If this Magicland business took over, the army would do something drastic. 'There may be only eleven of us, but we'll – we'll blow up the Public Conveniences, or something.'

Well!

As the Duchess observed, it was just one of those days. One of those days when you don't know whether to go out and be run over by a bus, or stay in and be decapitated by a flying saucer falling through the roof.

In came old Uncle Adolphus with a wicked smile on his face. 'Guess what's just crashed through the roof?'

Everyone held up their hands in horror. (Luckily he was only joking, but it was a nasty moment).

'How much?' he said, gleefully. 'What's it fetch, this Magicland, and when do we get it?' And he twiddled his hearing aid so as not to miss a dollar of it.

'It's only a rumour,' they explained to him, very loud. (Good heavens, who started these rumours?) 'We don't know *what's* happening until we find the document.'

'Oh.' Uncle Adolphus, disappointed, turned down his hearing aid.

But it was too late to stop the rumour now. No matter how you shoved it down in one place, up it popped again, faster than ever, in another place – like a beach ball in a swimming pool. People were turning up at the Palace from everywhere, trying to ring the doorbell, banging on the door, mouthing at the window. . .

'What's this about dollars for Diddlesdorf?' asked the manager of the Grand Railway Hotel.

'When's this Mr Shekelburger coming?' demanded the owner of the Diddlesdorf Nite-Spot.

'Money for Magicland?' inquired the Craft Co-operative hopefully.

'We should be eligible. . .'

'Is this where we put in a claim?'

The Tourist Board arrived, all three of them, jabbering away all at once, eyes popping with enthusiasm. 'Is it true?'

'. . . marvellous opportunity! Never get another chance like this. . .'

'. . . make Diddlesdorf a household name. . .'

'. . . Magicland! We'll be the richest gnomes in Europe!'

Viscount and Viscountess Lobe arrived, all two of them.

'Isn't it WONDERFUL!' breathed the Tourist Board.

'No,' said the Lobes, sourly. 'We're disgusted. It ought never to be allowed.'

'But. . .'

'The whole of Diddlesdorf clogged up with enchanted castles and magic forests! Nincompoops going round dressed up as fairies and witches! What *is* this country coming to?'

'Exactly so!' agreed the Duchess vigorously.

Squeals of protest from the pro-Magicland people. Shrieks of disagreement from the anti-magic faction. Both lots started to shout at once. The Duchess's sitting-room (which was now only standing room) was beginning to sound like the monkey house at the Zoo – or even a House of Commons debate.

On either side of the coffee table, the two sides prepared for battle. With the Duchess were General Storr and the two Lobes. Facing them were the Tourist Board and their allies the hoteliers, the ice-cream sellers, people from the night-clubs, the Craft Co-operative, the Hoverrug Service, the restaurants, old Uncle Adolphus and all. In the middle stood P.M. like a miniature referee without a whistle. 'We don't *know*. . .' she kept saying, to anybody who looked as though they might listen. 'We don't know yet if it's true. We don't know if there'll *be* any. . .'

But nobody heard a word.

Into the middle of all the hullabaloo barged the Gram Tam. All the commotion stopped at once – what was happening? Had he got any news?

'Um. . .' The Gram Tam looked vaguely round. 'Er, hello,' he said to the enormous crowd of people squashed into the sitting-room. 'Anybody ordered a taxi?'

'No. Why?' they said.

'Because there's some taxi-driver fellow at the door. Can't remember his name. . .'

'A taxi-driver!'

'Has he got the document?'

'. . . bringing the document?'

'. . . let him *in* then!'

'Bring him *in*!!'

The unfortunate taxi-driver, a small man with large glasses, was hauled into the sitting-room, and put before the Duchess.

'Now my good man,' she said. 'Have you got the document?'

'Well – no, ma'am.'

'NO!'

'Well, ma'am, it had Mr Schikleburger's name and address on it. So I posted it back. . .'

'You sent it back to Texas!'

'Yes, ma'am.'

Dead silence all round.

'But I did get a photocopy first. . .'

As shyly as wasps at a jam sandwich, the whole crowd lunged and squirmed to get a peep at the copy. The Duchess grabbed it first. She seemed to be reading so slowly. . .

At last she looked up. 'Well, Percival,' she said, 'You were right about one thing!'

'Er – yes, dear?'

'You certainly did sign an agreement to make Diddlesdorf into Magicland.'

'Oh, er – good.'

'By next summer.'

'Oh, yes?'

'But Mr Schickenburger's company isn't an airline, or a tour-operator, or a travel agency. It's an advertising company! They propose to advertise this – Magicland.'

'Oh. Um. . .'

'And they're not paying us a penny. *We* are paying *them*,' – the Duchess spoke very slowly, to drill it well in – 'THIRTY THOUSAND DOLLARS!'

The Gram Tam of Diddlesdorf was not an especially quick-witted chap. But he was a nifty mover when he saw a man-eating tiger staring him in the face – and there seemed to be one looking at him now.

4

The MOB, the MESS and the SPAM

It was a funny sort of day for a Tuesday, even by Diddlesdorf standards. Every hour or so, Diddlesdorf Radio broadcast a sort of guess-the-news bulletin. A spokesman from the Palace, usually Secretary Fizzell, would come on and say something, and all the listeners had to guess what was really happening. It was quite easy.

For instance, Fizzell said that the Gram Tam hadn't signed anything, and there was no document. That meant there *was* a document, and that the Gram Tam had signed it. Fizzell announced that there were absolutely no plans to advertise Diddlesdorf as Magicland. That meant Diddlesdorf would be advertised as Magicland. Fizzell confirmed that there was *no* crisis: that meant there *was* a crisis. And so on.

By late afternoon, even the woolliest-headed Diddlesdorfer had got the idea that there was something going on.

Well – what?

Ah! I'm glad you asked that question. Well, roughly speaking, the Gram Tam was dreaming up magic gasworks, magic railways, magic income tax, and goodness knows what – while the Duchess was working out ways of putting a stop to all magic. The hotel owners were planning to lure more tourists in – while Viscount Lobe was campaigning to keep all tourists *out*. The Tourist Board were adding up all

the money they needed to spend, and Secretary Fizzell was devising ways of not spending any money.
The Wizard was being told to hurry up with the
magification, and stop all this magification nonsense at once. And Peony Moondrop, having been
asked to do six impossible things before breakfast,
had put up a notice on her office door – 'Gone
Deep-Sea Diving'.

Well, that was Tuesday.

Wednesday was just as bad. Thursday was definitely worse. The Gram Tam and the Duchess were
not on speaking terms, and had to have all their
arguments in sign language. Fizzell was threatening
to resign if anybody spent another penny on anything *at all*. The Wizard was going around in ear-
muffs. P.M. was advertising for a job as an
astronaut. Oh, and Uncle Adolphus was learning to
play 'The Star Spangled Banner' on the piano
accordion.

Into all this muddle strode the lofty Duke of Potshotts. 'Got it!' he barked. 'Got the solution!'

'Really?' they said, astonished.

'Yes. Came to me this morning – walking the
dogs.'

'No! Really?'

'Simple idea – can't imagine why I didn't think of
it before.'

'Yes?'

'Dig a dashed great hole in the ground. . . .'

'Yes –'

'. . . and bury it!'

Stunned silence. On top of everything else, the
Duke had gone bananas.

He hadn't, as it turned out. He was still talking

about the rubbish tip. (You remember that little problem with the municipal rubbish?). The Duke, apparently, was the only man in Diddlesdorf who hadn't heard a *word* about the Gram Tam's deal with Mr Schickenburger.

'Where on earth have you *been*?' they asked him.

'Playing Monopoly,' he replied.

Whereupon Mr Wilkes the Wizard had the best idea he'd had for months. The Duke of Potshotts was easily the richest man in Diddlesdorf. What if. . . ? Offering to explain everything, Mr Wilkes took the Duke by the arm, and led him away into a quiet corner.

Thursday evening, and things had reached an all-time low. The army was threatening a coup, the Duchess was threatening to join them, and General Storr had locked himself in the lavatory and refused to come out.

Even the cat had left home, and gone to live next door.

Patiently, Mr Wilkes went round to everyone in turn, coaxing, cajoling, persuading. Finally, he enticed them all to a meeting, to listen to his new plan. (All but the cat, who refused to have anything to do with him).

'We're stuck with it,' he said. 'The document's signed – we can't unsign it now. Diddlesdorf is going to be advertised as Magicland *whatever* we do. So we might as well do it properly. . .'

Roars of fury from the anti-magic camp.

'. . . and do it BIG. Make it spectacular! Something to attract people from all over the world, thousands of them. That way, we'll make lots of money. After all, we've *got* to pay Mr Schickenburger. Thirty thousand dollars – we can't get out of that. . .'

'We'll be bankrupt!' screeched the anti-magic lot.

'Ah, but we won't,' said the Wizard. 'Because the Duke's going to pay.'

Suddenly, the whole business looked quite different. They all sat silently gulping and taking it in.

'You mean. . .' they said, 'the Duke's going to lend us. . .'

'Thirty thousand dollars,' nodded the Duke, 'on one condition! *Nobody* puts a rubbish tip in MY SAFARI PARK! Understood?'

'Right!' they gulped.

'And *nobody* pesters my lion!'

'Right!' they gasped.

'And then,' said the Wizard, 'when Magic has made us all rich, we can pay the Duke back again.'

It was an offer that even the Gram Duchess couldn't refuse. Well, she conceded, if the Duke was going to put up the loan, and Magic was going to pay it off, she supposed. . .

'CONGRATULATIONS! Marvellous – *marvellous* news!' In tumbled the Tourist Board, heartily shaking hands with everybody in sight.

'You've been listening at the door!' accused the Duchess.

'Oh no, ma'am, no, ma'am,' said the Tourist Board hastily. 'We were just, um, tying our shoelaces, just outside. . . Oh, this is wonderful news, wonderful news!'

Mr Wilkes was feeling disgustingly pleased with himself. He went round his Wizard's bungalow humming silly tunes, and grinning at himself in the mirror whenever he passed it. 'Any little problems? – just hand them to me!' he crooned to the computer.

In fact, he was so pleased with himself that he even wrote to his mother.

'And the beauty of it is,' he wrote, 'that it solves all the arguments at once, not just the money side. At last we've got everybody working together on it – well, *nearly* everybody. Though I don't know whose silly idea it was to call us the Magical Organization Board. You can imagine what we get called for short!'

Yes, Mr Wilkes was pleased with himself, and pleased with the MOB. He was even pleased with the MESS they made (Magical Entertainments Scheme, of course – what did you think?).

Ah, poor foolish fellow! He thought he'd solved all Diddlesdorf's problems in one fell swoop. Unfortunately, he'd forgotten the two worst ones. The first problem was the Gram Tam. And the second – well, that didn't become clear until a little later.

Still, for the time being, the magification of Diddlesdorf seemed to be going wonderfully well. More and more people were eager to join the MOB. Ideas started flowing – gushing, in fact, like water from a burst pipe: the whole Board was getting *drenched* with Ideas. Some of them were even put into effect.

Within three weeks, boring old Diddlesdorf was definitely showing signs of magifying. I don't know about the Romance and Adventure, exactly, but for the man in the street the whole business was certainly a Mystery. Most Diddlesdorfers vaguely imagined magification as a few concrete garden gnomes dotted here and there. They were in for a shock.

Overnight, traffic wardens turned into witches. Or at any rate, they were all issued with witches' hats and cloaks. School uniform disappeared, and kids turned up as dwarfs and fairies. The tatty old Tourist Information Kiosk vanished, and in its place appeared a little marzipan house! (Plastic marzipan, but – oh! – it did look sweet). And people couldn't believe their tongues when the big new fountain in Mulberry Square started spouting fizzy lemonade!

The Gram Tam, of course, was insufferable. He kept bouncing about, and beaming in people's faces, which was very worrying – it made you wonder if you'd got ketchup on your nose, or something. 'Exciting, isn't it?' he'd say, and bounce away again .

'Exciting, isn't it?' he beamed at Secretary Fizzell. Fizzell looked disgusted. 'Exciting, eh?' tried the Gram Tam again.

'Extremely, sire.' And Fizzell's mouth curled slightly at the ends, like an elderly cheese sandwich.

By now Fizzell seemed to be about the only person in Diddlesdorf who hadn't joined the MOB. The MESS was coming along nicely. They'd organized pension schemes for street minstrels, and royalties for giant-slayers.

'But we haven't got any giants,' objected the Gram Tam.

'We're *coming* to that,' they said.

'Right,' said Uncle Adolphus, who had elected himself chairman, 'That's next on the agenda – Giants and Dwarfs, hiring of. Any progress on that front?'

'Well, I've been in touch with a couple of dwarfs,' said P.M., 'and a giant who doesn't mind pretending to be slain – for a fee. Old acquaintances of mine, you know – from the circus.'

'Ah, circus! Right!' said the Gram Tam, cottoning on. 'Well, offer them a good salary. Ask 'em how they'd like to settle down. They'd get an inflatable pension, tell 'em.'

'Inflation-proof, I think, sire.'

'What? Are they?'

'No, I mean the pension, sire. Inflation-proof pension.'

'Well, all right – that as well.'

'Excellent, excellent!' said Uncle Adolphus. 'Can we move on to Damsels in Distress and Knights Errant. Mrs Cronko, I think you've been dealing with those?'

'That's right,' said Mrs Cronko (of the Craft Co-operative). 'I start interviewing on Monday.'

'And have you had a nice lot of applications?'

'Plenty of Damsels in Distress! Seven hundred and ninety three of them. . .'

'Yes – and how many Knights Errant?'

'Four.'

'Oh dear.'

General Storr was tapping away busily at his pocket calculator. 'Means each Knight'll have to rescue a hundred and ninety eight and a quarter Damsels,' he said. 'They should manage that. Given time.'

'Oh, there's no time limit on the rescuing,' said the Chairman.

'Only thing is,' said the Gram Tam, 'er, what will they do with a quarter of a damsel once they've rescued her?'

They all hurried on to the next item, in case he started making jokes about headquarters, hindquarters, married quarters, or anything else. They got through six whole items before the Gram Tam's attention wandered off on its own, and came back with something unexpected.

'A Dragon!' he announced all of a sudden, and made everybody jump. 'A Dragon – that's what I want. I *knew* there was something, if only I could think of it.'

'Oh, er,' they said nervously. 'A Dragon. How very nice.'

'What *size* of Dragon,' inquired Mr Goldmark, the Bank Manager. 'What size of Dragon did you have in mind, sire?'

'Oh, you know. . .' The Gram Tam waved his arms about to indicate something roughly the size of Milton Keynes. 'Don't want to do these things by halves, you know. Half a loaf, I always say, er . . . gathers no, um . . . broth. Is it?'

Now clearly the Duchess should have nipped this Dragon in the bud – or wherever Dragons spend their early infancy. But, alas, she didn't. She was out of the room when it first reared its head, and only found out about it far too late. By then the monstrous beast had, as it were, a foot in the door.

After that, there was no stopping it. Every time the Gram Tam opened his mouth, it was Dragon,

Dragon, Dragon – wouldn't it be terrific to have a Dragon, when could the Wizard start on the Dragon, hadn't they always *wanted* a Dragon?

'Couldn't you just wait, sire,' they said, 'until we've got these ogres and things sorted out?'

The queue of prospective ogres and things looked round hopefully, waiting to be sorted out.

'Good Lord,' said the Gram Tam. 'How long has *this* lot been here?'

'If you think *this* is a long queue,' they said, 'you should see the queue for the Castlette Conversion Grants!'

He certainly should. It was driving everyone round the bend. Even the most energetic MOBsters were feeling a bit daunted by the queue for Castlette Conversion Grants. It had all started off as such an innocent little idea, thrown in at the end of a meeting.

Diddlesdorf, as somebody pointed out, was full of houses. Thousands of houses, all very ordinary and boring. Why didn't they get people to convert their houses into magic Castlettes? You know, turrets, battlements, drawbridges, and things? It would make the place look much more interesting. More like Magicland!

'So how can we do it?' they said.

'Well – offer them grants. . .'

So they did – and it worked. It worked appallingly well. The Housing Department didn't know what had hit them. The very first morning the grants were on offer, they opened the doors . . . and were squeezed like lemons in the crush. Eventually, the queue stretched all the way along the corridor, down the stairs, into the street, along the pavement, and round the corner past the fish-and-chip shop. ('Ye Cods and little Haddocks!' gasped the fish-and-chip man in astonishment. 'We're not open yet! Not open yet!' he mouthed through the window. 'We're not queuing for you,' mouthed the queuepersons cheerfully.)

'This is getting out of hand!' declared the Duchess. 'We need more help with this magification.' And she marched along to see what Secretary Fizzell was doing.

'We need some help,' she said. 'It's high time you joined the MOB, Fizzell.'

But, much to the Duchess's surprise, Fizzell flatly refused. 'Certainly not!' he sniffed. 'We can't all primpse around like Goldilocks and the three bears. Somebody sensible has to run the country.'

The Duchess was quite taken aback. 'Fizzell!' she seethed, 'In Diddlesdorf, *I* am the judge of what is and isn't sensible.' And she turned on him a look as black as a thundercloud at a cricket match.

But it did no good. Fizzell would have nothing whatever to do with any of it. Not the MOB or the MESS, or anything. He just sat there, looking like a plate of boiled cabbage. *Very* sensible.

Meanwhile, Castlettes were spreading like wildfire. Everybody wanted one. It was all they talked about. 'Have you converted yet?' – 'Oh, we're being turreted tomorrow. . .'

Decorators and D.I.Y. stores had never seen business like it. Anybody who looked remotely like a builder was liable to be grabbed in the street and hauled off to construct battlements. Semis sprouted towers. Big detached Castlettes appeared with flags flying; whole rows of terraced Castlettes got their

54

own mini-portcullis; bungalows were moated and drawbridged; and blocks of flats were topped with turrets and ramparts. Meanwhile the 'Diddlesdorf Echo' was reporting the dangers of pouring boiling oil on the postman. . .

Poor Mr Wilkes was run off his feet. Not only did he have to approve all these Castlette plans – he was also having trouble with his genies. He had invented, you see, a cunning scheme for replacing all the pedestrian crossings with magic lamps. You rubbed the magic lamp, and a big green genie told you when it was safe to cross the road. From the side, it was a big red genie, stopping all the traffic. (All done with holograms, of course).

'How's it doing?' asked P.M. one day. 'Need any help?'

'Well, the green genies are doing their stuff, but, oh dear, these red genies,' sighed the Wizard. 'They put a hand up – and it falls off!'

'Oh dear,' said P.M. 'What a blow!'

'Besides,' he muttered, 'I keep getting this awful feeling – that they're *listening*. Or somebody's listening. . .'

'Listening?'

'Yes, listening. And watching. Watching what I'm doing, through the window, or something, when I'm not looking.'

'Oh, not to worry,' soothed P.M. 'You're just cracking up. Happens to us all now and again. You need a holiday!'

'D'you think so?'

'I certainly do. You've deserved it. I'll ask the Gram Tam right away.'

'Oh, my giddy aunt!' Mr Wilkes grabbed his beard and winced. 'That reminds me – I meant to go to the library, and look up the specifications for Dragons. . .'

It was dark when he finally left the library that night. A fine rain was coming down steadily, and almost everyone else had gone home.

Mr Wilkes hurried down the quiet street, and glanced across the road at the big dark window of the Co-op. 'Giant Sale!' said the window, in dim fluorescent lettering, 'Inflatable Giants – half the marked price!' But what was that? He thought he caught a glimpse of something, reflected in the window. Someone following him. . .

'No, no,' he thought, 'it's just me. I'm cracking up.'

And he turned into the alley by the bank. But what was that sound? Footsteps? Surely not. . . No, no: he was cracking up, just as P.M. said. It couldn't be. . .

'AAGH!' – Mr Wilkes nearly jumped out of his skin.

A huge, bald fellow in a pale green body stocking had sprung out of the shadows and grabbed his arm. He had a sort of leopard skin round him. 'Mr Wilkes!' he hissed.

'Blimey!' muttered Mr Wilkes. 'We finished interviewing ogres *last* week.'

'I'm not an ogre,' said the pale green fellow plaintively. 'I'm an elf.'

'Oh – sorry.' Mr Wilkes flicked anxiously through his diary. 'The elves are coming, er, Wednesday after next.'

'Just a quick word,' whispered the elf urgently, pulling him back into the shadows. 'Listen – they've got it in for you!'

'Eh?'

'They're after you. I gotta warn you. You'd be better out the country. . .'

'Who. . . ?'

'The SPAM,' whispered the elf. 'The dreaded SPAM!' And away he loped, and disappeared into the darkness.

5

Trouble with Socks, String, and Noxious Beasts

Every morning, after breakfast, the Gram Tam clambered up the steep little stairs to the box-room in the loft. There was a narrow window there in the eaves, the highest window in the Palace. From it, he could gaze out over his realm, his noble Land of Magic – well, he could see as far as the allotments, anyway, if it wasn't foggy.

He could also see part of Castle Street, the roof of the Bank, a big block of offices with TO LET in window-high letters across its blank face, and the back wall of the magistrates' court. Now that was a most interesting wall, an informative wall. The Gram Tam liked to read its graffiti: he had binoculars especially for it. His favourite one was written in pink paint and said:

'Tomorrow has been CANCELLED owing to lack of interest.'

He laughed at that one every time. But one morning, the wall had an even better one for him. To his delight, it said:

'MAGIC RULES, O.K.'

He read it out loud: 'Magic Rules, O.K.'

The next day another one appeared underneath, declaring –

'Magic Rules are made to be Broken.'

The Gram Tam didn't quite know what to think about that one.

He was still thinking about it, on and off, when

the Public Cleansing Department came along on his bicycle, and scrubbed them all off. But the wall didn't stay naked for long. That very night, an unknown person sneaked up with an aerosol paint can, and sprayed in great ugly black letters:

'SPAM'

and –

'SENSIBLE PEOPLE AGAINST MAGIC!'

SPAM? Sensible People? Never heard of them! Still more worrying was a huge scrawl that said:

'SMASH THE MAGIC – YOU KNOW IT MAKES SENSE!'

The Gram Tam went straight to the Duchess and told her. 'Disgraceful!' he said. 'Disgraceful – daubing public walls with this, er, claptrap. Isn't it? Eh?'

'Well, Percival,' said the Duchess. 'If you don't like graffiti, you should make them illegal.'

'Ah! Er . . . well, I don't know about that, exactly. Some of them are rather good. There used to be one about "Tomorrow has been cancelled. . ."'

'That reminds me,' said the Duchess. 'Talking of cancellations, I've had to cancel all my engagements for this afternoon. That means you'll have to do the opening of the Sports Hall yourself.'

'Ah – er, Sports Hall. This, er. . .'

'Take Mr Wilkes with you. He'll remind you what you have to do.'

'Wilkes – ah! Yes, he's a good chap, Wilkes. Why can't you come? You're good at opening things.'

'I really *must* go to the dentist. I've been trying to get there all week.'

'Oh, no problem! You just go straight out of

here, turn left, down the road and . . . er, . . . yes.'

Mr Wilkes, meanwhile, was struggling with a Dragon. True, it looked very like any other circuit-board to the naked-eye, but it was called 'Dragon' on the front of its notebook. Whatever it was, it was giving the Wizard endless trouble.

'Oh, bother,' he muttered, and peered at the circuit diagram

'Oh, blast!' he said, and frowned at the oscilloscope.

'O-oh KLOPSTOCK!' he yelled – and in walked Secretary Fizzell.

'Ah, Wilkes.' Fizzell put on a rather rancid smile. 'Just popped in to see how things were coming along.'

'Really,' said Mr Wilkes. Since when had Fizzell been interested in how the magic was coming along?

'Still dreaming up little toys for His Exigency, are we? What's it this time –' Fizzell picked up the Wizard's circuit-diagram book and read the front cover. 'Mm – a dragon, eh? Very interesting. *Very* interesting. . .'

Fizzell handed back the book. Mr Wilkes slapped it on the desk and glared at him.

'I hear you're off on holiday?' Fizzell went on.

'Yes,' said the Wizard.

'Feel you need a break.'

'Yes,' said the Wizard.

'Doesn't do to work too hard at this magic, you know,' said Fizzell. 'You'll be seeing little green men, before you know where you are!' And he giggled unpleasantly as he poked around at the other notebooks on the shelf. 'Well, must be toddling along. Don't want to disturb your great thoughts any longer, do we?'

'No,' said the Wizard.

'Oh, by the way,' said Fizzell, as he was leaving, 'His Exigency wants to see you. Immediately.'

'Oh, bother,' sighed the Wizard, when he'd gone. 'Hey diddle diddle! I hate Fizzell!'

The Gram Tam was sitting in his study, watching a pile of important papers from a safe distance. He looked anxious.

'Oh, er – Wilkes,' he said. 'Tomorrow's cancelled. I mean, um . . . Muriel's having her feet done. At the dentist. . . No, er. . . Anyway, we're opening a Sports Hall. This afternoon.'

'Oh really, sire?'

'Yes – can you pop along there? Give me a bit of support and er. . ?'

'You do remember, sire, don't you, that I'm going away on holiday this afternoon?'

'Oh, um. . . Where. . . ?'

'Well, a little place in France, actually.'

'France! Oh, well – you could go there via the Sports Hall. Same direction. . .'

So there it was. Whether he liked it or not, Mr Wilkes was meeting the Gram Tam at three o'clock, at the Sports Hall.

His fingers tightly crossed, the Wizard turned up at the new Sports Hall at ten to three. At the door, he met the Sports Hall Committee, all in their very best track suits and trainers, a selection of moderately important people in Sunday best and soft shoes, and a crowd of enthusiastic sports fans. (You could see that they were sports fans: they tended to jog-on-the-spot when they got bored.) They chatted pleasantly and waited.

'His Exigency insisted on arriving by himself,' explained Mr Wilkes. 'He wanted to make a grand entrance on his Hoverrug.'

'I do hope,' said one of the Committee, with a tactful little cough, 'that His Exigency remembers the soft-soled shoes. Our new Hall has a very special floor, and we're very proud of it.'

'I did remind him,' said Mr Wilkes, and kept his fingers firmly crossed.

At three o'clock, who should appear on his Hoverrug but the Gram Tam. He had arrived, at the right place, at the right time, *with* the notes for his speech.

Wearing football boots. With studs.

The entire Sports Hall Committee gazed at the boots in horror. They looked at one another. They looked at Mr Wilkes. They looked down at the boots again.

'Er – borrowed some football boots.' The Gram Tam proudly surveyed his footwear. 'For the sports and, er, so forth.'

While the by-standers giggled behind their hands, the Committee whispered something to Mr Wilkes. Mr Wilkes whispered to the Gram Tam. The Gram Tam looked down at his boots, puzzled.

'Why *not*?'

Again Mr Wilkes whispered in his ear.

'Damage the floor! I'm not going around with an axe, am I?'

'Perhaps, sire,' murmured one of the Committee politely, 'Perhaps you could simply remove your boots. Come and do the ceremony in your socks.'

The Gram Tam whispered to Mr Wilkes. Mr Wilkes whispered to the committee.

('What's he say?' whispered the crowd to one another.

'He says he's got holes in his socks!' somebody whispered back.)

Chuckles broke out all round, and the Committee muttered urgently about what to do next. Mr Wilkes bobbed back and forth between the Committee and the Gram Tam. Somebody would have an idea: somebody else would slap it down; somebody would start to rush off; somebody else would call him back. . .

The Wizard slipped into the hall to have a look at the plaque that the Gram Tam was supposed to be unveiling. It was covered with a little blue curtain, with a cord to pull it back. Ah! He seemed to have thought of something. More jabbering away behind hands, and somebody was sent to fetch a ball of string.

So this was the plan! Everybody was to go outside and listen to the Gram Tam's speech. Then, while everyone else went into the Hall, the Gram Tam, outside, would pull the string that would pull the cord that would open the curtain that would unveil the plaque that would declare the Sports Hall open.

Simple!

No, no . . . it wouldn't work. The plaque was at the wrong angle to the door; you couldn't pull the curtain open that way.

Through the window then! The Gram Tam could pull the string through the window – but, oh dear, the windows were too high.

Somebody else was being sent to fetch something. There was a clattering and bumping, and yes – yes, a ladder was appearing up at the window. The Gram Tam was being sent up the ladder with the ball of string; the string was being unwound, down through the window, to be tied to the cord, that would pull the curtain, that would unveil the plaque . . . and so on.

No, no – another snag. Now that the Gram Tam was up the ladder, nobody could hear his speech. A loudhailer, then – they'd got a loudhailer somewhere. Someone was carrying it up the ladder, and people were being shepherded back into the Sports Hall. Everything was ready. The Gram Tam was going to make his speech, through the open win-

dow, with the loudhailer, before pulling the string
. . . and so forth.

Marvellous!

Everybody gathered round the plaque and
looked up at the window. The Gram Tam, glasses
on his nose, holding on to the ladder with one hand,
his notes and the string with the other, started to
make his speech.

He was very pleased to have been asked to open
this magnificent Sports Hall, he said, and it was a
magnificent Sports Hall, and he was quite sure a lot
of work had gone into it, and a great many people
were to be thanked for the part they had played and
so on, and so on, and it was a magnificent Sports
Hall, and he declared this magnificent Sports Hall
open.

In front of the plaque, the curtain twitched, and
remained firmly shut.

'I declare this magnificent Sports Hall. . .'
boomed the Gram Tam, with a hint of desperation –
'Sports Hall OPEN!'

On the word 'Open', the curtain shivered a little –
and stayed shut.

'Wilkes!' came a fierce whisper from up at the
window. 'The blasted *string's* stuck! On the thingy –
the window catch. . .'

'Wait, sire!' called Mr Wilkes, and rushed out to
help. 'Don't do anything until I get there!'

But it was too late. The Gram Tam reached in
through the window to untangle the string – and got
two fingers caught in the ring of the window catch.

'Wilkes! I've got my confounded fingers
caught. . .'

Whereupon they had to call the Fire Brigade to rescue the Gram Tam from the window catch. And the Fire Brigade arrived with a ladder to put up inside the Sports Hall, but of course they couldn't go in, because they weren't wearing soft-soled shoes. . .

Diddlesdorf was in stitches. People were rolling about with laughter as they watched the nine o'clock news. And next morning, when the papers showed photos of the Gram Tam, with string, being rescued by the firemen, in socks, it all looked even funnier.

But by then, Mr Wilkes was well out of the country. He was sitting in the French sunshine, eating French food and drinking French wine. For a whole fortnight Diddlesdorf, as far as he was concerned, might have been on some other planet.

So he never knew anything about the rumpus that was going on there. He didn't hear about the leaflets that turned up all over Diddlesdorf, showing the Gram Tam stuck at the top of his ladder, with the words 'Would you let this man open *your* Sports Hall? JOIN THE SPAM!' He didn't see the posters demanding 'MORE SENSE – LESS MAGIC'. He was peacefully ignorant of all the furious rows that followed, until the Duchess had the whole lot confiscated, and the Mayor put them all on a big bonfire in Mulberry Square. ('Daren't take them to the Rubbish Tip,' he said. 'No room!')

No, the Wizard knew nothing of all this – yet. He got back to Diddlesdorf, with a souvenir hat and a suntan, on the Saturday afternoon. On his way home, he'd worked out a cunning little plan for getting those infernal red genies to work properly. So he took out the Magic Lamp circuit, and got down to work.

At half past six, Mr Wilkes noticed the time. 'Crikey!' he said to the clock. 'It's half past six!' (Which was a silly thing to say to a clock, especially as it was the clock that told him in the first place). 'I promised I'm meet P.M. in the Laundrette at six!'

Off he rushed to gather up his dirty socks and shirts, glaring at the clock as if it were the clock's fault. He arrived at the Laundrette breathless. It was ten to seven: Peony Moondrop, bless her heart, was still sitting there behind a large plastic bag of tumble-dried clothes.

'Oh good!' she called, jumping up as he came in. 'Did you have a nice holiday? Super! – now you put your things in this machine, and we'll switch on. We don't want anyone to hear what we're saying.' She leaned forward and whispered very fast.

Mr Wilkes didn't hear a word. 'You what?'

P.M. peered cautiously around the Laundrette in case there were any spies in the washing machines. Everyone else had packed up their clean linen and hauled it off home. 'The SPAM! Have you heard about all this nasty business with the SPAM?'

'Funny you should say that,' muttered Mr Wilkes thoughtfully. 'A big green elf warned me about that. . .'

P.M. looked at him anxiously. 'Are you sure you had a good holiday?'

'Oh, you know,' said the Wizard quickly. 'Just a chap dressed up as an elf. What is it – this SPAM?'

'It's very sinister,' whispered P.M. vehemently. 'It's all a nasty plot. . .'

'A nasty what?' whispered Wilkes.

'A nasty *plot* – against magic.' And P.M. explained how the Sensible People had suddenly sprung up out of nowhere, and nobody knew exactly who they were. How they were ferociously

anti-magic. How they'd put out advertisements and leaflets, saying they would cut out the MOB, the MESS, and the Wizard altogether.

'Cut me out!' whispered the Wizard. 'Sounds painful! Why are we whispering?'

'In case *they*'re listening!' whispered P.M., and she clutched her big black handbag tightly, to stop any secrets falling out.

'And how about everybody else – the ordinary people? Have they all gone Sensible?'

'Oh no, no, no. Lor' lubaduck! When they realized the SPAM were against Hoverrugs and Castlettes, nobody was interested.'

'Well, that's all right, then!'

'Oh, dear no – no, it isn't. They may not have much support, but they've got *lawyers*. Expensive ones! They reckon they can prove that magic is against the law.'

'But that's stupid!' laughed Mr Wilkes. 'Magic – against the. . .'

'Shush. . .' whispered P.M., and glanced suspiciously over her shoulder. A woman was looking in at the door.

'Thought I left some pyjamas here,' said the woman, and went away again.

'*She* might be Sensible,' whispered P.M. 'For all we know! Now, about that Dragon. You haven't mentioned it to anybody else yet, have you?'

'Er. . .'

'Because they reckon it's illegal to bring Dragons into Diddlesdorf. Or at least, that's the rumour I heard.'

'Dragons!' said Mr Wilkes ruefully. 'What's the punishment?'

'Forty days and nights in the Gram Tam's dungeons.'

'But he hasn't got any dungeons, has he?'

'Oh, I dare say the SPAM can get around that.

70

Even if they have to build the dungeons specially.'

Mr Wilkes gazed gloomily at his washing as it churned round and round like an upset stomach. 'Well, that's marvellous, that is! If I don't make His Exigency a Dragon I'm in the dog-house, and if I do make it, I'm in the dungeons! What's a poor Wizard to do?'

'He's not to worry!' said P.M., and patted his shoulder soothingly. 'You just get on with your Dragon, but keep very quiet about it. Nobody will know it *is* a Dragon until it's finished. By then, we'll have this all sorted out.'

Mr Wilkes looked doubtful.

'We will – you'll see', said P.M., picking up her big bag of clean clothes and slinging it over her shoulder. 'It'll all come out in the wash! Toodle-oo.'

Mr Wilkes thought about the SPAM and the magic all the way home. The more he thought, the more he worried.

Was there somebody, besides the MOB, who knew about the Dragon? Yes! Of course – Secretary Fizzell!

No, no, he thought, don't be silly. Secretary Fizzell was a pain in the neck, but he *couldn't* be a Sensible Person. The Gram Tam's own Private Secretary, secretly working against the Gram Tam? Impossible. With any luck. . .

Mr Wilkes took out his front door key – and stopped. There, in the letter-box, was stuffed a piece of paper. He pulled it out, and looked. It was a note, short, neat, and type-written.

'Dear Mr Wilkes,' it said,

'We don't want Wizards in Diddlesdorf. You get out, or we'll get *you*.
    Yours sincerely,
        The SPAM.'

6

The Sensible People, the airing cupboard, and other horrors

The Lord High Steward was reviewing his dahlias. He had just spent a happy hour strengthening the fortifications – pellets to keep the slugs off, upside-down flowerpots on sticks to keep the earwigs off, insecticide to keep the greenfly off, fungicide to keep the mildew off, threads of black cotton to keep the birds off. . .

Suddenly, 'Aa! Aa! Aa!' he brayed and flailed his arms frantically. . . But too late. Trampling across his dahlias was the one pest for which no-one had yet produced pellets.

'Hello!' waved the Gram Tam cheerfully.

'Excuse me a moment, Your Exigency,' said the Lord High Steward. And he ran to the potting shed, shut the door quietly behind him, and said a rude word. Then he came out and wished the Gram Tam a very good morning.

The Gram Tam was still trampling around on the dahlias, helpfully putting the stakes upright again. 'I'm er, I'm a bit worried,' he confided, 'A bit worried about this Dragon. The Wizard, now – he'll be back from his hols now, won't he? How d'you reckon he's getting on with it? This Dragon? Eh?'

'Well, sire,' said the Steward, 'You could go and ask him.'

'Er . . . well – ask the Wizard, you mean? Well, I've wandered over there, but you know, it's a bit off-putting. All that mob outside – they might. . .'

It appeared that the Gram Tam had been scared away from the Wizard's bungalow by a mob of people outside; he wanted somebody to go with him. So off trudged the Steward with him, silently lamenting his ruined dahlias.

Outside the bungalow, there was the mob – five protestors and six reporters, making eleven in all. The reporters chattered away like starlings, bobbing about and peering in the windows. The protestors stayed on the pavement, quiet as zombies. Each protestor held a placard grimly above his head, and paced up and down in front of the bungalow in a kind of solemn, silent Highland reel. Only their placards said anything:

'MAGIC IS BAD FOR YOU'
'SUPPORT THE SENSIBLE'
'OUT WITH OGRES'
'WE HATE HOVERRUGS'
and –
'WEED OUT WIZARDS!'

Round and round in dead silence they walked, looking at nobody. It was quite eerie.

'Take no notice, sire,' said the Lord High Steward, and walked straight through them to the front door. The Gram Tam followed; the reporters crowded round.

'Is it true, Your Exigency. . .'

'Is this the end of the Wizard?'

'. . . put an end to magification?'

The Gram Tam looked around helplessly.

'Tell them to go away, sire,' said the Steward.

'Oh, er . . . go away!' said the Gram Tam.

'Yes, Your Exigency,' said the reporters, and moved back a yard or two. The Gram Tam and the

Steward nipped round the back and sneaked in through the back door.

'Hullo!' they called. 'Hullo!'

'I'm in here,' came a small muffled voice from the airing cupboard.

'He's in there,' said the Gram Tam, opening the cupboard door and shutting it again.

'Well, shouldn't we ask him *why*, sire?' asked the Steward.

'Um. . . Why are you in there, Wilkes?' asked the Gram Tam, opening the door again.

'I'm hiding,' said Mr Wilkes.

'He's hiding,' said the Gram Tam and closed the door again.

The Lord High Steward had a go. 'You can come out now, Mr Wilkes,' he said. 'It's only a few lunatics from the Sensible People.'

'It's not them I'm worried about!' came the muffled voice from the cupboard.

'What then?'

'This!' – and a very worried-looking hand slid round the cupboard door, clutching a long, quivering envelope.

The Steward took the letter gingerly between thumb and finger, hoping it wouldn't explode. It didn't. He unfolded it cautiously. It didn't notice. He read it through.

'Mother of God!' he said, when he had finished. 'Holy Smoke! Strike me down!' And he handed the letter to the Gram Tam, who was trying to read it over his shoulder.

'*Good* heav . . . *Good* gra . . . Good Lord!' said the Gram Tam as he read the letter. 'Er . . . um . . . er. . .'

'We'll have to smuggle him out of here, sire,' said the Steward. 'Hide him somewhere in the Palace until we can see a lawyer about it. A lawyer, now – a lawyer will know what to do.'

'A, er . . . a lawyer – er,' said the Gram Tam, hopelessly flustered. 'Lawyer him out. Er . . er . . . a smuggle. Er . . . smuggle him, um. . .'

The Steward took hold of the Gram Tam, stopped him spinning aimlessly round and round, and tried to calm him down. 'Now sire, it's altogether simple. It's just a matter of getting Mr Wilkes out of here without anybody seeing him go. We just need to put our heads together.'

The Gram Tam tried very hard to put his head together. 'Look here, Wilkes,' he said. 'You're a Wizard, aren't you? Eh? Can't you make yourself invisible – or something?'

Mr Wilkes couldn't.

'Well, er – how about that lot outside? Make them invisible?'

Mr Wilkes couldn't do that either.

'I've got it, sire!' said the Steward, clapping his hands to his scalp to keep his idea in. 'The dustmen! The dustmen come this morning. Look, sire, we can smuggle Mr Wilkes out in a dustbin, and they can take him away in a dustcart.'

'But I'll be chewed to bits by that big grinder thing in the back,' wailed Mr Wilkes. 'I'd rather be fed to the Sensible People!'

'No, no! – dear me, not at all,' said the Steward. 'You'd hop in the cab at the front, with the dustmen. We'll give them a little something, for their trouble.'

So off they went, the Steward and the Gram

76

Tam, to look for the dustbin. The Gram Tam tried the bedroom, and came back with no success. The Steward looked outside the back door, and returned with a big brown dustbin bag. Hurriedly, they tried to bundle the Wizard out of the airing cupboard into the bag. His head and shoulders wouldn't go in at all. They tried pushing him down hard. The bag split. They tried picking the bag up — and couldn't lift it so much as a millimetre.

'Tell you what!' said the Gram Tam. 'Let's put some real rubbish in the bag.' And off he went to find some real rubbish from the kitchen pedal-bin.

'But – the Wizard, sire!' said the Steward anxiously. 'What do we do with him?'

'Oh, you know. . . He can carry it.'

It was not everyone who saw the point of this. Nevertheless, Mr Wilkes was thrust out, bemused, carrying his split bag of rubbish.

'Ah, Mr Wilkes,' said the reporters. 'We see you've hastily packed your belongings in a paper bag.'

'Yes,' said Mr Wilkes wearily.

'Are you being sent into exile?'

'Yes,' said Mr Wilkes.

'Where to? Siberia?'

'Yes,' said Mr Wilkes.

So that was the story that got into the papers. It put everyone off the scent for days.

'Mummy! Mummy!' Wisteria burst into the sitting-room with the other girls close behind her. 'Mr Wilkes is in the hall and he's got a bag and Daddy wants to hide him in the rubbish. . .'

'Not in the rubbish!' corrected Winifred. 'In the *Palace*.'

'No, he's *disguised* as the rubbish. . .' said Wanda.

'What *is* all this rubbish?' demanded the Duchess, and she stalked into the hall to find out.

'Ah! Muriel – where can we hide this, er, Wizard?' asked the Gram Tam.

The Duchess stared at Mr Wilkes's haggard face and leaking bag of rubbish.

'Must do something *quickly*, ma'am,' urged the Steward. 'We've got the SPAM after him!'

And with much ado, the poor Wizard was chivvied upstairs and into the spare bedroom. 'I demand to know what all this is about!' called the Duchess after them, and hurried to investigate.

'About this, ma'am!' The Steward waved Mr Wilkes's letter at her. 'Look – from the lawyers, Shybald and Squelch. It's altogether terrible: look here!'

The Steward read the terrible letter out loud:

'Dear Mr Wilkes,
We would draw your attention to a certain article of the Law of Diddlesdorf, enacted in 1572, in the time of the fourteenth Gram Tam. According to this law,

"If any subject of the Gram Tam do procure, or cause to be shewn, any public spectacle. . .

blah, blah, blah. . .

of a magical or conjuring nature, upon a Holy Day, or upon any Feast of any Saint in the Diddlesdorf Calendar. . .

blah, blah, blah. . ."'

'What *do* you mean – blah, blah, blah?' said the Duchess crossly. 'Whatever is all this about?'

'It means, ma'am, that anybody who does any magic on a Saint's Day gets clobbered. By law. Look – it says here, ". . . shall be branded on the forehead in the manner of a common criminal, and afterwards banished from the realm of Diddlesdorf for ever."'

'Branded on the forehead! Banished! What is all this nonsense? You haven't been doing magic on Saints' Days, have you, Mr Wilkes? Which days are they, anyway?'

Mr Wilkes shrugged ruefully while the Steward waved several sheets of foolscap paper over his head. 'Here's the list, ma'am – Saints and their Feast Days. The lawyers sent it.'

The Duchess took the list – and nearly fell through the floor. And no wonder! The sheer weight of sanctity on that list was enough to crack the floorboards. St Boniface and St Botolph, St Chrysostom and St Polycarp, St Fiacre, St Ubald, and St Willibrord. . . One hundred and seventeen saints: not a saint less! One hundred and seventeen saints in the Diddlesdorf calendar, or one every 3.12 days – the Steward worked it out on his pocket calculator.

'They've got us, ma'am,' said the Steward, 'pinned and wriggling.'

'We are not insects,' said the Gram Duchess, 'and we are not beaten. Call the Prime Minister! I refuse to be stabbed in the back by one of my own laws!'

'Oh, deary me!' said P.M. when they showed her the letter and the list. 'Oh, deary me! Oh deary me!' She hopped from foot to foot in agitation. 'I *knew* this would happen! Where did they get it from? I've never heard of this stupid old law!'

'Oh,' said the Duchess, 'it's one of those useless ancient ones we don't use any more. I always meant to give them to a jumble sale. . .'

'We've got to do something quickly!' urged the Lord High Steward. 'Because if we don't, d'you see, and these fools get young Wilkes prosecuted – why now, they might prosecute any of us! That law could do for us all. We're all in the same magic boat!'

'Good Lord!' said the Gram Tam suddenly. 'A

magic boat! What a marvellous idea! Wilkes, could you make us a magic boat, d'you think – after the Dragon, you know. . .'

'Percival!' thundered the Duchess, 'Mr Wilkes won't be able to make you anything at all if you don't put your mind to this! If we don't find a way out – a loop-hole – you can forget the Land of Magic once and for all.'

'Got it,' said P.M. who had been thinking hard. 'The Gram Tam made the law – or rather his great-great-great-great-great-whatever grandfather did. So surely the Gram Tam can repeal it. Then we'll be rid of it altogether.'

'Good idea,' said the Duchess. 'Off you go, Percival. Go and repeal this law!'

'Er, er . . . repeal?' spluttered the Gram Tam. 'Good heavens, Muriel, I haven't repealed a law for donkeys' years! I can't, er . . . I can't, um. . .'

But the Duchess was not to be deterred. If these so-called Sensible People could hire lawyers to bring these fusty old laws out of oblivion, *she* could hire lawyers to put them back again. 'They'll be finding old laws to ban Hoverrugs next!' she exclaimed. 'Not to mention ogres, and magic lamps, and Castlettes, and. . .'

'Dragons?' the Gram Tam quavered in horror. 'Not Dragons!'

'Oh, no doubt!' said the Duchess.

So the Gram Tam rushed off to look up how to repeal laws.

'No-one must know that Mr Wilkes is here,' ordered the Duchess as she left, 'Until we've got legal advice on our position. No one! Not even the servants.'

81

So the Wizard vanished. Or at any rate, he was locked in the spare bedroom, and nobody else was allowed in. P.M. fed him on Mars bars and little cellophane packets of cheese biscuits, with plastic cups of tea, secretly, from the Palace vending machine.

Sometimes he lay on the bed; sometimes he sat on it. Sometimes he sat on the floor, and wished he'd never been a Wizard. 'I'd rather be a sub-atomic particle physicist,' he thought, 'or even a sub-atomic particle!'

'Cheer up,' said P.M. as she waltzed in with yet another cup of hot robot-beverage. Then she told him the good news. They'd got some lawyers on it – and it was thumbs up. All that the Gram Tam had to do was to proclaim publicly that the old laws didn't apply any more. And that was it.

Mr Wilkes sipped the anonymous brown liquid doubtfully, and waited for the bad news.

The bad news, said P.M., was that, just at the moment, they didn't seem to be able to lay their hands on the laws. . .

'You mean, you've lost them.'

'Never fear! We'll find them – they *must* be in the Palace somewhere. . . Golly! What's that?'

It came from the corridor: bellowing, shrieking, stamping of feet.

A riot, perhaps? No, it was the Gram Tam and the Duchess, having one of their little disagreements.

'*You* put them away – you ought to know where they went!'

'I never touched them! *You* put them away. . .'

'Stuff and nonsense! You had them last, when we redecorated the study, and you said. . .'

'You said to put them in the loft. . .'

'Percival, *will* you listen to what I'm *saying* – we took them *out* of the loft when we put the new insulation in. . .'

'No we didn't! We. . .'

'Yes we did!'

'We didn't!'

'We did!'

'We didn't!'

('It sounds,' sighed P.M., 'as though I'd better go and do some diplomacy.')

Mr Wilkes sat on the floor, hugging his knees. He wondered whether this was going to be a full three-hour quarrel, or whether there was any chance of finding the laws before bedtime. What if the SPAM got in? What if they took him away? What if. . .

There seemed to be a cease-fire in the corridor. P.M. was doing her stuff. By the sound of it, she was persuading them to try looking in the cupboard under the. . .

'They're not *there*,' wailed the Gram Tam. 'I've *looked* in there.'

'Where, sire?'

'In the, you know – cupboard under the stairs.'

'No, no, sire: I was going to say, in the cupboard under the attic stairs – the little one.'

'Aah!'

'Of *course*!'

'I *told* you they weren't in the loft! Get the key, Percival.'

'You've got it. . .'

'Don't be ridiculous; you know perfectly well that *you've* got it.'

'I haven't!'

'You have.'

'I haven't.'

'You have!'

The quarrel started moving off downstairs, in search of the key. Mr Wilkes sat on his hands to stop himself biting his nails. Suddenly, a sound of small footsteps scurried along the corridor.

'Ma'am! Sire!' P.M. was calling from the top of the stairs. 'The cupboard's open! You don't need the key!'

Mr Wilkes took his hands out again so that he could cross all his fingers.

Sounds of feet racing up the stairs again.

'Impossible!' declared the Duchess. 'That cupboard is always kept locked!'

'Kept locked, you know,' said the Gram Tam. 'On account of the, er, valuables – you know, old laws and things.'

'But it's unlocked now, sire. Come and see!'

Mr Wilkes crept to the bedroom door to listen, as the footsteps hurried along the corridor to the cupboard at the end.

What now? Were they there? Had they got them? Why were they all so *quiet*? Had they been eaten? Had they fallen through a hole in the floor?

'OH! NO!!'

P.M.'s face appeared, apologetically, round the bedroom door. 'Sorry about this, young Wizard,' she said. 'Looks as though you've got a long wait!'

7

The Spy in the SPAM!

'Burglars! *Real* burglars?' Wisteria was quite excited. 'What – here? Last night?'

'Burgulars, burgulars! We got burgulars!' chanted Wilhelmina and Wendy.

'What did they burgle?'

'Some of Dad's papers,' said Winifred. 'Some boring old laws, or something.'

'Whatever would anyone want those for? Hey, Wanda – they're *my* tights!'

'No, they're not. Look, they're marked at the top – W for Wanda.'

'No, you moron! That's W for Wisteria.'

'No, it's not. It's M for Medium – upside down.'

As it turned out, the tights were too small for either of them, and were marked W for Wilhelmina.

'Same old argument,' sighed Winifred. 'Why they couldn't have called us Anna, Brenda, Clara, Dora and Elsa I can't imagine.'

'Boring!' said Wanda. 'You sound just like old Fizzell.'

'"Why we cannot adopt *sensible* policies, I can't imagine,"' mimicked Wisteria. '"This magical nonsense is all very well. . ."'

'"But somebody's got to run the country!"' they chorused all together.

'Poor old Fizzell,' Wisteria giggled. 'He's trying to reform and be nice.'

'*Fizzell*!'

'Mm. He gave Wendy a packet of jelly babies yesterday. Didn't he, Wen?' But Wendy had run off. 'For being a good girl, *she* said.'

'Did he now?' said Winifred thoughtfully. 'I wonder what she did to deserve that?'

The Gram Tam felt worried. Things were getting out of hand. The Palace had been burgled and his moth-eaten old laws stolen; the key to the attic cupboard had gone missing – gone to visit the others in Texas, for all he knew; Aunt Arabella wanted to come and stay, but he couldn't let her into the spare bedroom because he was hiding a Wizard in there; the Wizard couldn't get on with his Dragon because he was being hidden in the spare bedroom; and on top of all that, these horrid Sensible People were trying to put a stop to his magic! They even had the nerve to put another leaflet through his door. Just as the Duchess had confiscated the last lot! 'Magic costs Money,' said this nasty leaflet. 'Stop the Magic,' and stuff like that. Why? What had he done to *deserve* all this?

He was just pondering upon injustice, the meaning of life, and so forth, when Secretary Fizzell came in. 'Have you remembered about tomorrow, sire?' asked Fizzell.

'Yes, of course I've remembered,' said the Gram Tam irritably. And that was another thing: he was tired of people quizzing him on his general knowledge. 'Of course I've remembered. Comes after today.'

'I mean, sire, have you remembered what's happening tomorrow?'

'Oh – the usual disasters, I dare say. Plague of locusts? Earthquake? Something like that?'

'No, sire. I'm going away on holiday.'

'On holiday! Now! You, er. . . Good Lord, Fizzell, why didn't you *remind* me?'

'That, sire, is what I'm doing now.'

'Oh, er. . . Er, well – how am I going to manage?'

'As you usually do, sire. Ineptly.'

(The Gram Tam didn't know what that meant, so he didn't argue.)

'Before I go, sire, we'd better clear up one or two matters outstanding.'

And Fizzell set to on the matters outstanding, which turned out to be the usual boring old financial stuff – taxes, public expenditure, money supply, economic growth forecast. . . Fizzell read it all out solemnly, while the Gram Tam read the 'Star Trek Annual'. Every so often, Fizzell would put down a piece of paper on top of the annual, place his fat finger on a dotted line, and say, 'Sign here.' And the Gram Tam would do as he was told.

'Ah, Muriel!' he said, when the Duchess walked in. 'Is it lunch-time?'

'Lunch-time!' retorted the Duchess. 'Here we are in the middle of a crisis – the ancient laws of Diddlesdorf stolen from under our noses, the entire magification under attack from a group of Sensible lunatics – and all you can think about is lunch!'

'Well, I'm hungry. I've had a hard morning doing the economic, er, thingy.'

'Just one more signature, sire,' insisted Fizzell. 'It's the latest policy document on the Municipal Refuse Facility.'

'Ah – Municipal Refuse, um. . .' said the Gram

Tam. 'Don't tell me! Something to do with, um, buses – no! – picnic tables – no! New loo in the Town Hall!'

'No, sire.'

The Gram Duchess sighed heavily, and explained for the hundred-and-forty-seventh time that a Municipal Refuse Facility was a rubbish tip.

'Oh. Oh, that. What are we going to do about it, then?'

'Well, sire, this just goes to prove, yet again, the utter incompetence of that useless Wizard. We asked him *weeks* ago to provide a magic Refuse Facility, and he has totally failed. . .'

'But he can't, you know!' said the Gram Tam. 'He's hidden in the sp . . . er, he's, um, in . . .'

'*Indisposed*,' said the Duchess firmly. 'Mr Wilkes is indisposed.'

'Well, ma'am,' said Fizzell, with a smile wrapped round his face like a particularly affectionate boa-constrictor, 'he's failed to come up with a Facility, whatever the reason. So, as the matter is becoming *pressingly* urgent, I suggest a new approach to the Duke of Potshotts.'

'Absolutely not,' said the Duchess. 'You know perfectly well that we made a firm agreement with the Duke. His safari paddock is *out*.'

'You made an agreement, ma'am,' said Fizzell, 'but I didn't. Why don't you just leave the negotiations to me?'

'But you're going on holiday,' said the Duchess.

'And so is the Duke.'

'Oh, I don't think that need hinder us,' smiled Fizzell, and he gathered up his papers to leave.

'Before you go,' said the Duchess, 'when did you last see the key to the attic cupboard? The police want to know if it was lost before the break-in.'

'Oh, I've no idea, ma'am,' said Fizzell.

'None?'

'None at all. I really haven't time for such trifles. After all, *somebody's* got to run the country.'

It was the rush hour in Diddlesdorf – though quite why it was called the rush hour it's hard to say. Nobody *rushed* anywhere. Fumed, yes, fretted, hooted and swore, certainly; but rushed? No chance. The traffic managed about as much movement as a blocked drain. Every car, Hoverrug and bus that got sucked in, got stuck in. And that was that.

Through the middle of the muddle, slipping in and out like quicksilver through any little sliver of a gap, came a large black bicycle.

'Watch out!' people shouted as it shot past. 'There goes Peony Moondrop!'

Suddenly, she whisked through to the inside lane, leapt off the bike, and left it snuggled beside a Hoverrug.

'Holy Smoke!' cried the Lord High Steward from the front door of the Palace. 'You'll be had up for dangerous driving before you're much older, P.M.'

'Oh deary me! I'll put in for my Cycling Proficiency Test tomorrow!'

'How d'you get on? Any luck?'

They hurried inside, and shut the door. P.M.

90

nodded hard. 'This very evening,' she whispered. 'Six o'clock. Here's the address. . .' and she gave the Steward a little note. 'Is he ready – our spy?'

'He's raring to go,' whispered the Steward. 'To-night it is, then!'

Seven o'clock, and P.M. was still hard at work at her desk in the tiny office. By half past seven she was beginning to glance at the clock. Eight o'clock – he still hadn't come back. Had he been eaten? Had he been converted?!

Ten past eight: there was a tap on the door. . .

P.M. picked up the phone. 'Is that you, Steward? He's back – and it's on!'

'Something important to say? Now?' The Gram Tam had sneaked off for a quiet game of snooker, by himself. He felt he played better by himself. (He always won, by himself.)

'Yes – this minute,' said the Duchess. 'The Prime Minister has some important news about the break-in.'

So the reluctant Gram Tam was removed from the snooker room to his study.

'Now, P.M.,' said the Duchess. 'What are these shocking revelations? What have you discovered?'

'Some very interesting answers, ma'am,' said P.M.

'Oh, er – do we know the questions?' asked the Gram Tam.

'Yes, sire. First of all, how did the SPAM know about those stupid old laws? Nobody's used them for centuries. Nobody's even opened them since the clear-out when the old Gram Tam retired!

'Second, who stole the laws – and who's got them now?

'And third, where did the key to the attic cupboard get to?'

'It appears to me,' observed the Duchess, 'that if we knew the answer to the third question, we should know them all. Because whoever had the key must have stolen the laws, and whoever stole the laws must have told the SPAM about them.'

'Exactly, ma'am!' P.M., triumphant, couldn't help bouncing on her heels. 'And we know who has the key!'

The Gram Tam, impressed at the brilliant detective-work going on around him, nodded so hard that his glasses fell off. 'Hang on a minute!' he said. 'I can't see what you're saying. . .'

When he found them, the Lord High Steward was pushing forward a shy second-housemaid to say her piece.

'Now, Polly,' said P.M. 'Tell us about the key to the attic cupboard.'

'Um,' said Polly, 'I put it on the key-ring with them spare keys. Them that were in the tea-pot.'

'You're quite sure?' asked the Duchess.

'Yes, ma'am. You said to hide it somewhere. Well, we kept forgetting where we'd hidden it. So we put it in there. Well, course, them keys went to Texas.'

'Now we'll call our second witness!' said P.M. And in came Winifred, bringing her little sister Wendy.

'Come on, Wendy,' she said. 'Tell Mummy and Daddy what you told me.'

Wendy, overcome with so much grown-up attention all at once, squirmed and giggled. 'I got some jelly-babies,' she announced.

'Go on. Who gave them to you?'

'Mr Fizzell gave them to me, and it was last week, and the postman came, and I opened the door, and he said there was a parcel for Daddy from Texas, and Mr Fizzell came up behind me and he said he'd take the parcel, and he opened it, and it was keys. And he gave me a big box of jelly babies for being a good girl and not telling anybody and pretending there wasn't any keys come. Only I finished them all now anyway!'

And off ran Wendy, squealing with laughter.

'And that was the day before the burglary,' said P.M. 'Now for our third witness. Come in, third witness!'

In walked a young man in a dark suit, clean shirt, and tie, with brown hair neatly parted at the side. The Gram Tam felt he'd seen him before – somewhere. . .

'Freddi!' exclaimed the Duchess.

'My godfathers!' said the Gram Tam. 'What's gone wrong with your hair? It used to be, um, purple.'

'At last,' said the Duchess. 'You've seen the error of your ways. You look *much* better without safety pins!'

'It's me *disguise*, ma'am,' protested Freddi. 'I'm disguised as a Sensible Person.'

When they had got over their hysterics at the notion of Freddi as a Sensible Person, they asked him what had happened.

'Well,' said Freddi, 'I infiltrated, didn't I? I went along to one o' these SPAM meetings, and pretended to join 'em.'

'And?'

'I sussed 'em. What they're up to, why they wanted them laws. . .'

'So the SPAM have got them laws – er, those laws!' – even the Duchess was losing her grip on grammar. This was all rather exciting. 'And Fizzell?'

'Oh, yeah, Fizzell's in it – up to here!' And it all came out, how Fizzell had stolen the laws and given them to the SPAM, how their lawyers were working on them to see what other mischief they could do. . .

'You mean, they've got other ideas!'

'They'll get their teeth in all of us if they can,

ma'am. That won't just be Mr Wilkes hidden in the spare bedroom. . .'

'*All* of us!' quavered the Gram Tam, horrified.

'Monstrous!' thundered the Duchess. 'How dare they? And how did *you* know that Mr Wilkes was hidden in the spare bedroom?'

'*All* of us!!' the Gram Tam hissed like an over-heated pressure cooker. 'ME and everybody? Muriel – I'm putting my foot down – I'm not having it – I'm going straight round to those lawyers tomorrow morning, and I shall . . . I shall . . . I shall . . . DO something! That's what I'll do. *All* of us! In the spare bedroom!'

Sad to say, the Gram Tam's fighting mood didn't quite last out the night. Next morning, he wouldn't get out of bed. When the Duchess tried to get him up, he pulled the bed-clothes over his head and complained of a sore throat, or a headache, or a pain in his foot. . .

'Don't be ridiculous,' said the Duchess crisply. 'You're going to see these lawyers. Hurry up!'

'But I, um . . . I, um . . . What am I going to *say*? What am I going to *do*? What if they say no!'

'You simply say exactly what I tell you.' And with much ado, the Gram Tam was bullied out of bed and made to get ready.

So there they were – the Gram Duchess, the Gram Tam, the Lord High Steward, Freddi and Rick the footmen, and the Deputy Head Gardener (a strapping great lad, who looked as though he might deal with a dozen lawyers with no trouble) – one by one, creaking up the narrow stairs to the lawyers' office.

'Is this the right place?' asked the Gram Tam anxiously, when he got to the top.

'Of course it is,' said the Duchess. There wasn't much doubt about it: 'Shybald & Squelch: lawyers' it said on the door.

'Announce us, footmen!' ordered the Duchess.

So Freddi and Rick walked straight in and announced, loudly – 'His Exigency the Gram Tam, and the Gram Duchess' – to a startled typist.

'Ooh!' she squeaked. 'Ooh! Ooh!' she dithered.

At that moment, from their inner lair beyond the typist, out came Shybald and Squelch. They both wore grey suits, gold-rimmed glasses and thin grey hair. Apart from the fact that one was twice the height of the other, there wasn't much to choose between them.

'Your Exigency. Ma'am,' they said, smiling and bowing. 'What can we do for you?'

'I . . . um, er, um. . .' spluttered the Gram Tam.

'. . . demand that you return my laws,' whispered the Duchess at his ear.

'. . . demand that you return my laws!' said the Gram Tam.

'. . . at once!' whispered the Duchess.

'At once!' said the Gram Tam.

'But, sire,' said Shybald and Squelch, 'we know nothing about any laws!'

'Oh. Er, well, um. . .'

'Yes you do!' whispered the Duchess.

'Do I? Oh, oh yes. . . Yes you do!' said the Gram Tam.

'No, sire, we don't,' said Shybald and Squelch.

'In that case,' said the Duchess out loud, 'we

shall come and search your office.' And into the
inner lair they marched, all six of them. They sorted
through, searched along shelves, peered into cup-
boards. . .

'This desk drawer's locked,' said Rick.

'Tell them to unlock it!' whispered the Duchess in
the Gram Tam's ear.

'Unlock it!' whispered the Gram Tam, very loud.

'I'm afraid we've lost the key, sire,' said Shybald
and Squelch.

'Unlock it at once. . .' whispered the Duchess.

'Unlock it at once. . .'

'. . . or we'll take the whole table!'

'. . . or we'll take the whole baby!' gabbled the
Gram Tam.

'. . *table*!' hissed the Duchess.

'. . *table*!' roared the Gram Tam.

'Ah!' said Mr Shybald (or was it Squelch?) as Freddi and the Deputy Head Gardener moved menacingly towards him. 'I've, um, just found the key in my shoe. Fancy that!'

And under six pairs of watchful eyes, he drew out the key, and unlocked the drawer.

And what do you think? There they lay, bundled and neatly tied with red ribbons, like a secret hoard of nasty birthday presents. The ancient laws of Diddlesdorf!

8
Where's that Fizzell?!

'You just wait – ' fumed the Gram Tam, stomping up and down the sitting room. 'You just *wait* till that Fizzell gets back! You just wait. . .'

'Percival,' said the Duchess wearily, 'will you sit down and stop treading on these laws! We're trying to sort them out. You don't even know what to do with Fizzell when he does get back!'

'I shall . . . I shall . . . You'll see! You just *wait*. . .'

Meanwhile, P.M., Winifred and the Duchess had the laws laid out all over the floor. There were fifty-seven of them – all quite useless.

'What codswallop!' chuckled P.M. 'How did they *think* of them all?'

'Goodness knows why we kept them,' said the Duchess. 'All the good laws are in a tea-chest in the study.'

'You just *wait*. . .' growled the Gram Tam.

'Daddy, sit down!' said Winifred. 'You nearly trod on my fingers. Oh, here it is! This one about doing magical things on Saints' Days.'

'And here's the one about "noxious beasts",' said P.M. 'Oh dear, oh dear!'

They made a curious collection. There were laws against spitting in church, selling love-potions without a licence, putting spells on other people's cows, and using the Gram Tam's palace for 'entertainment or public spectacle'. In the end, they decided to repeal the lot. There was just one little law that took the Gram Tam's fancy. It was to forbid anyone 'molesting the Gram Tam's Griffons'. But, as Winifred pointed out, since nobody knew what the Gram Tam's Griffons were, somebody might molest them by accident. So that one had to go too.

'You just wait till Fizzell gets back!' muttered the Gram Tam.

'Time for the Proclamation,' said the Duchess. 'Percival, are you ready?'

'Er, yes . . . er . . . what do I have to do again?'

The Duchess explained, for the fourth time, that the Herald would go out into Mulberry Square, announce what was going to happen, read the laws out loud, and ask the people if they had any objections. 'Then you must say, "I repeal these laws," and the Herald puts up the notice to say that they're cancelled.'

'Right! Er, . . right! Um, what happens if somebody *does* object?'

'Then you must listen. Listen to their objections. They're your subjects, and your subjects' views should always be taken into account. Unless, of course, their views happen to be wrong. Now, you will remember. . .'

'Yes, yes – "I repeal these laws."'

It turned out a lovely afternoon for the Gram Tam's Proclamation. The sun shone, the band played, and the Herald stepped out in all his finery.

Well, anyway, the Steward dressed himself up as a Herald and went out looking moderately silly. Mulberry Square was full of people going home from work, and several of them stopped to have a look.

'Nice for October, isn't it?' said the Mayor's wife to the other official guests.

Hardly anybody disagreed.

'I repeal these laws. . .' muttered the Gram Tam under his breath.

'Where is he?' boomed a large voice from behind the by-standers. Striding forward came a tall dark thundercloud of a man. 'Where's that FIZZELL?'

'Ah – the Duke of Potshotts,' said the Gram Duchess. 'How very nice to see you! So glad you could. . .'

'Where is he?! Just wait till I get my hands on him!'

'Now, your grace, the problem is, we're just having a Proclamation. *Do* you think this could just wait until. . .'

'Where *is* the bounder?'

'He's on holiday – he's not here, and the Herald is just. . .'

'On holiday! Do you know what he's DONE?'

Suddenly, at a nod from the Duchess –

BLAA-AARP!

– the Herald made an appalling noise on a sort of trumpet. The crowd jumped out of their skins.

BLAA-AARP!!

'All right, all right! I can take a hint,' said the Duke. 'Let's have this Proclamation then.'

So the Steward – sorry, the Herald – started proclaiming.

'His Exigency the Gram Tam of Diddlesdorf declares before his subjects, the people of Diddlesdorf, on this fifteenth day of October nineteen hundred and eighty six, that, um, he's fed up with some of his old laws and wants to get rid of them.'

101

'Herald – really!' scolded the Duchess. 'You could have put it better than that!'

The crowd tittered.

'Sorry, ma'am,' said the Herald, and tried again.

'. . . that, um, certain laws, being now obsolete, are to be repealed. These laws are as follows. . .'

More and more people were drifting up to see what everyone was looking at. Hoverrugs were piling up at one side; cars were parked on double yellow lines.

'What's he saying?'

'Something about some old laws. . .'

By the time the Herald came to the one about not putting spells on cows, the people at the front were starting to laugh. They chuckled over the love-potions; were killing themselves over the noxious beasts; and there was one about 'consorting with naughty vagabonds' which for some reason had them all in hysterics.

When the Herald had read solemnly through all fifty-seven of them, he blew his trumpet again.

BLAA-AARP!!

'If any person have any objection to the repealing of these laws,' he announced, 'let him speak now!'

People giggled and looked at one another. Now what? Was that the end of the show?

'Just a minute!' boomed a voice, unexpectedly.

Everybody turned to look. It was the Duke of Potshotts.

'I object!'

'Eh?'

'I object to the repealing of one of those laws.'

'What?'

'That one about not using the Gram Tam's Resi-

102

dence as a place of entertainment. How does that go again?'

'Er,' said the Herald. 'Er, – Anyone who allows or causes any part of the Gram Tam's own Residence or Palace to be used for the purposes of entertainment or public spectacle. . .'

'Yes!'

'. . . is a gross disturber of the Gram Tam's peace.'

'That's it. That's the one. We'll keep that one.'

And away strode the Duke of Potshotts, while everyone called, 'Eh? What for?' after him.

Nobody seemed quite sure what to do next. P.M. and the Duchess got into a huddle with the Mayor and one or two other people, to discuss it. Then they borrowed a pencil, crossed off the law about the Gram Tam's Residence from the list, and pinned it up on the notice board anyway.

'That'll do,' they said.

The Gram Tam waved at anybody who seemed to be looking.

The band played 'Knees Up Mother Brown', and one or two other pieces they knew.

People started to wander away, and that was that.

'Thank heaven for that!' said the Duchess. 'At *last*, we can have our spare bedroom back!'

When Mr Wilkes was finally freed from the spare bedroom, there was great rejoicing, and an impromptu party to celebrate. They invited everybody who turned up.

'Leave a note for the Duke,' suggested P.M. 'Perhaps he'll come along later.'

It was quite a decent party. They had an ogre telling funny stories, and a fairy playing 'Nymphs and Shepherds Come Away' on the tuba. They also had party hats, and a trifle, out of packet for quickness.

P.M. demonstrated the tablecloth trick – and it *very nearly* worked. (Only the remains of the trifle fell off, and landed on the cat, who spent the rest of the evening in silent indignation under the sideboard, licking it off). The Lord High Steward sang an Irish song, and remembered half the words. And Mr Wilkes showed off his magic biro. (It did invisible writing).

It was the sort of party where people laugh at anything.

They even laughed a bit when the Gram Tam told, for the fourth or fifth time, the story of how he rescued Mr Wilkes from the airing cupboard, and hid him from the SPAM in the spare bedroom.

'Dead lucky the SPAM didn't turn up today!' said Uncle Adolphus. '*They* would have objected to the Saints' Day law being repealed. Then we should have been in a mess.'

'Oh, we thought of that,' replied the Duchess. 'Or rather, P.M. did.'

'Simple, really,' twinkled P.M. 'We just advertised a SPAM meeting – somewhere else! Besides, we took the precaution of locking their lawyers in the attic, so they couldn't tell anyone we'd got our laws back. Which reminds me – has anyone thought to let them out?'

(Of course, nobody had. So they set them free, and sent them home, tired and cross, each with a walnut whip.) At last, just when some of the less rampageous types were thinking it was time they went home too, Wilhelmina came galloping in squealing – 'He's here!'

'Who's here?' they said.

'Duke of Potshotts.'

'Oh, good,' said the Duchess. 'Now perhaps we'll find out why he wanted to keep that ridiculous old law about public spectacles.'

'Public spectacles?' asked the Gram Tam, looking vaguely anxious – and he hastily removed his own, in case they turned public on him.

'Ah, do come in,' said the Duchess as Potshotts appeared at the door. 'We were just wondering. . .'

'Where's Fizzell?' demanded the Duke.

'Oh, yes – you wanted Fizzell. He's on holiday at

the moment, but. . .'

'When's he coming back?'

'Next week. I'm sure we. . .'

'The cad! The rotten bounder! Just wait till I get my hands on him!'

'Funny you should say that,' observed the Gram Tam. 'Just what I've been saying. D'you know, I'm furious with Fizzell, too. Can't remember why, just at the moment – er . . . oh yes! Got it! D'you know what he's. . .'

'D'you know what he's DONE?' thundered the Duke.

'Er, no – er, what?'

'Got the bulldozers in!'

'In what?'

'In my safari park!! The moment my back's turned! Bulldozers, JCBs – about to dig a confounded great *hole*. Turn the whole place into a rubbish tip. . .'

'Er – refuse facility!' said the Gram Tam, looking pleased with himself.

'And,' growled the Duke, jabbing the Gram Tam in the chest, 'Do you know what he's done with my lion?'

'Er – sprayed it pink? Stuffed it? Had it with chips?'

'He's taken it to the Zoo!!'

'Oh, er . . . did it have a nice time? He could take it to the pictures next. . .'

And the Duchess hastily removed the Gram Tam – before he got brained, stuffed, and taken to the museum.

It took a long time and several glasses of lemonade to cool down the irate Duke. (P.M.

diluted the lemonade with gin, which helped.) Not to worry, they said, it would all be sorted out. They'd send the diggers home again. Yes, he could have his safari park. No, they hadn't forgotten the agreement. Yes, he could have his lion back. . .

Finally, everybody sat and listened politely while the Duke did his party-piece. It turned out to be his famous recitation from Shakespeare, a thrilling bit from Act Three of Two Gentlemen of Verona – or, come to think of it, was it Act Two of Three Gentlemen of Verona?

Well, whatever it was, one thing naturally led on to another. And they were all well into the fourth verse of 'She'll be Coming Round the Mountain When She Comes' when Rick the footman appeared at the door. He beckoned to the Duchess. There was a hasty whispered conference, and then the Duchess turned to the assembled company, with a grave face and bad news.

'Terrible news!' she announced. 'There's been a gigantic landslide.'

'What?!'

'It's the old Diddlesdorf Rubbish Tip. It's finally collapsed. Percival, there's going to be the most awful stink about this!'

9

How Fizzell fell into his own trap!

'So you see, Wilkes,' said the Gram Tam, flicking shampoo suds off a damp copy of the Diddlesdorf Chronicle. 'We can't just sort of sit around.'

'No sire,' said the Wizard, still dozy after his first good night's sleep for far too long.

'We'll have to, er . . . *do* something,' said the Gram Tam. 'You can see the scale of the problem!'

Indeed, you could see the scale of the problem. It covered the whole front page – a collapsed blancmange of fallen rubbish, photographed from the air, and over it, the glaring headline: 'Great Diddlesdorf Rubbish Tip Disaster'.

'The inevitable has happened,' read Mr Wilkes. 'The Diddlesdorf Rubbish Tip, dangerously over-burdened for years, has finally lost its balance. Two hundred and seventy four feet high at the last measurement, this mammoth pile has been the subject of controversy for years. On these pages we have often begged for action. Now it is too late. The Tip collapsed yesterday, burying two singing dwarfs and a magic banana.

'It took rescuers three hours to dig them out. . .'

'It goes on like that,' said the Gram Tam, dripping shampoo gloomily. 'And worse.'

'Yes, sire,' said the Wizard, 'But don't you think you should finish washing your hair?'

'What?'

'You seem to be halfway through washing your

hair, sire. You haven't rinsed the shampoo off yet.'

'Oh, er. . . Yes, but this blasted Tip. . . This rubbish. . .'

'Don't worry, sire. We'll think of something, somehow. I'll try very hard to make a Magic Rubbish Disposal System. But it'll take a little while. You'll easily have time to rinse the shampoo off first!'

'Oh, yes, er. . .'

'Look, how about doing it here?' Mr Wilkes pointed to the washbasin in his bathroom.

'What? A Magic Rubbish Tip in your bathroom?'

'No, sire – I mean rinse the shampoo off. . .'

'Oh! Oh, yes – right.'

When the Gram Tam had rinsed his hair, and rubbed his head a bit with Mr Wilkes's bath-mat, he reappeared frowning. 'Thing is, Wilkes, old Fizzell did say this would happen, and blow me – he's going to say, "I told you so!"'

'Never fear, sire, we'll have a new and better Rubbish Tip in no time. Just give me a week or two. . .'

'I mean to say, it's more than a fellow can bear – what with old Fizzell stealing our SPAM! er, laws, and er – and you just wait till he gets back! You just wait. . . . And then he comes and says, "I told you so". . . But Wilkes. . .'

'Yes, sire, I know, I know.'

'Thing is, it's awfully important, this new Rubbish Tip.'

'I know it is, sire.'

'I know it's important, this Tip. But this Dragon, now – you haven't forgotten, have you? The Dra-

gon? I mean, I know the Tip's urgent, but this Dragon. . .'

'Yes, sire, yes of course.' Mr Wilkes looked as
patient as a hundred and seventeen saints. 'Don't
you worry, sire. I'll make you a Dragon. *And* a
Rubbish Tip. Yes, yes – all at once! After all, what's
a Wizard for?'

For a whole week, Mr Wilkes shut himself in his
Wizard's Workshop, and worked, and worked, and
sweated, and worked. Unfortunately, his ideas
didn't.

Notes, circuits, diagrams, sketches were churned
out, screwed up and thrown away by the bucket-
full. The waste paper basket looked like a scale
model of the Diddlesdorf Rubbish Tip Disaster.

'Mustn't panic,' he said to himself – and started to
panic. Here it was, October already. Mr Schickenburger would be coming back in the summer, and
bringing all his advertising people. And what would
there be to advertise in Diddlesdorf? What would
they find?

A few damsels living in semi-Castlettes, Hover-
jams every rush-hour, and a collapsed rubbish tip!

Not to mention Sensible People scowling around,
finding fault with it all. Oh, it was all IMPOSS-
IBLE!

Maybe I'm in the wrong job, he thought earn-
estly. Would I be any good at drilling oil-wells?
Trout-farming? Conducting the London Symphony
Orchestra?

'What can I DO?' he typed in to his computer.

'Syntax error,' said the computer, unhelpfully.

So he went to see Peony Moondrop.

She was out. What's more, there was a note pinned to the door of her bedsitter; it said, 'Gone to see the Wizard'. So the Wizard trailed all the way back to his bungalow – only to find a note pinned to his door saying, 'Came to see you. You're out! Love, P.M.'

'I know what's the matter!' said Mr Wilkes to himself. 'I'm not a Wizard after all. I'm a rat in somebody's maze. And the somebody keeps moving the maze!'

Then he bumped into Peony Moondrop holding a large packet of chips, and changed his mind.

'Have you heard the news? Have you heard?' panted P.M., skipping about and offering him chips all at once. 'Fizzell's back from his holiday.'

'And what's happened?'

'Give you three guesses!'

'The Gram Tam's shaken him warmly by the throat.'

'No.'

'Old Potshotts welcomed him with open jaws.'

'No.'

'Give up.'

'He's been arrested! He's in a cell at the police-station.'

'Oh, they've made a mistake there,' said Mr Wilkes with a sigh. 'It turned out that it wasn't actually Fizzell who stole the laws – he just borrowed them, to show them to the SPAM. It was the lawyers who stole them, and wouldn't give them back. I heard all about it after. . .'

'No, no, no!' laughed P.M., throwing the bag of chips into the air and catching the lot, without dropping a chip. 'No, no – not for stealing the laws.'

'What for, then?' asked Mr Wilkes, puzzled.

'For hiring out the cinema!'

Now that really *was* unexpected. Mr Wilkes stood and gaped like a goldfish. 'Hiring out the cinema?'

'That's right,' chuckled P.M. 'You know the Cinema, next door to the Palace?'

'Yes, of course.'

'Well, you know that it was once the Palace ball-room and things, and that it was Fizzell who hired it out to be a Cinema? It seemed like a good way of making money. . .'

'Yes, but – that's not illegal, is it?'

'That's the funny thing about it! It never used to be. Or at least, nobody ever *knew* it was. Not until Fizzell and the SPAM got all those fusty old anti-magic laws out!'

'No! Don't tell me!' Mr Wilkes stood there with a chip halfway to his lips, too stunned to eat it.

'Yes, yes,' danced P.M. 'It's against one of those very laws. The one that says you're not allowed to use the Gram Tam's palace for the purposes of entertainment or public spectacle!' And she explained, as they walked along, how the Duke of Potshotts had decided to get his own back on Fizzell after Fizzell had tried to put the rubbish-tip in his safari-park; how the Duke had heard the law being read out, realized that a cinema was a public enter-tainment, and that Fizzell could be accused of that one, stopped it being repealed, and got Fizzell pro-secuted.

'So old Fizzell's dug a big trap. . .'

'. . . and fallen into it himself!'

'Whee-hee!'

And throwing the leftover chips to the pigeons, they raced to the Palace, howling with laughter.

'But what,' said Mr Wilkes, suddenly stopping, 'if Fizzell's actually found guilty of this, er, crime?'

'Ah!' said P.M. 'Well, the law says, the offender is to be thrown into the Gram Tam's dungeons for twenty years, and have his left ear cut off.'

'Golly!' said Mr Wilkes. 'What a terrible thought!'

It was a terrible thought. Secretary Fizzell was not a handsome sight at the best of times, and having his left ear cut off wouldn't improve him at all!

When they reached the Palace, they found everyone in a tizzy.

'Are you *quite* certain Potshotts won't change his mind?' demanded the Duchess.

'Not a chance, ma'am,' said General Storr. 'I've tried everything.'

'Then we shall have to have the trial immediately.'

'Oh, er . . . Good Gracious,' said the Gram Tam, who would have liked at least three weeks to dither about it. 'Trial? I, um . . . can't remember what you have to *do*, or anything.'

When it came to it, nobody in Diddlesdorf could remember how to do a real trial. 'It's years and years since we had a trial like this!' they said. 'We've forgotten what you have to do.'

Even the Gram Duchess got flustered about it. 'Where on earth can we hold it? What on earth am I going to wear? Who's going to do the judging?'

Now that was a good question. The ordinary magistrates said they couldn't possibly do it: they didn't know the words, and besides, they hadn't got the proper gear to dress up in.

'Er, look – didn't we used to have a proper judge?' asked the Gram Tam. 'What was his name – Codfish, or something?'

'Hake,' said the Duchess. 'But that was *years* ago, in your father's time. Justice Hake was decrepit even then: he'll be dead by now.'

'Ah! Er . . . well, could we borrow one? Does anybody hire judges?'

It was left to P.M., as ever, to sort out the problem. She put on her bicycle clips, bunched up her skirt, and cycled off to find a judge.

By the next afternoon, Justice Willibald Hake himself had been found, ancient but alive, in a high-class nursing home in the country. He looked as small and dry as a grass-hopper, propped up in his wheelchair with a rug over his knees.

'Would you like to do a bit of judging?' asked Peony Moondrop.

'Ooh, yes please!' said the judge, and he hopped out of his wheelchair, threw his rug over a passing rose-bush, and scuttled down the drive. His nursemaid ran after him, shouting to him to be sensible and come back at once. So he borrowed P.M.'s bicycle, and made his escape.

P.M. waved as he wobbled off along the road into town, and wondered what she should do next. 'I'll go and visit poor old Fizzell,' she said to herself. 'He'll be in a right old stew.'

She caught a Hoverrug straight to the Police Station. A policeman was just coming out of Fizzell's cell.

'Is he in a stew?' asked P.M.

'He's stewed, baked, boiled and sautéed,' said

114

the policeman, 'and now we're grilling him. All in all, he's not very happy.'

'Oh deary me! Perhaps I'd better pop in and see if he'd like a nip of gin.'

That evening in the Palace corridors, P.M. scurrying one way collided with the Wizard ambling the other.

'How's old Fizzell?' he asked.

P.M. made a little grimace.

'In a bad way, is he?'

'I think he's getting the heebie-jeebies,' she said. 'He was asking if you couldn't get him out of this by magic.'

'Crikey – he must be in a bad way!' said Mr Wilkes. 'He's never believed in magic before.'

'The sad thing is,' said P.M., 'I don't think he does now.'

Persuaded by P.M., Mr Wilkes went to see poor old Fizzell the next morning. The policeman let him into the cell, and locked the door on them both.

Secretary Fizzell was sitting with his tie undone on a bench in the corner. He looked wrinkled and saggy, like a balloon that's beginning to go down. Mr Wilkes felt quite sorry for him, and asked him how he was.

Fizzell didn't reply.

'Fizzell,' said the Wizard suddenly. 'Tell me something. Why have you hated me since you first set eyes on me?'

'Hmph,' said Fizzell, grumpily.

'Why have you done everything you could to make trouble for me?'

'I haven't.'

'And to make my magic go wrong?'

'I haven't.'

'And to get rid of me?'

'And to get the SPAM on to me, and get me arrested under one of these stupid old laws?'

Fizzell glared. 'Suppose I did?'

'Well, why? Why did you do it?'

'You know perfectly well why!'

'No I don't. Go on – tell me. I might be able to stop doing whatever it is you don't like.'

Silence.

'Besides, I *might* just be able to think of a way of getting you out of this mess. . .'

'You know what you did, you vile bully!' Fizzell scuffed the floor with his toe. 'Those teazles you used to stuff down my neck. . .'

'What!?'

'When we were youngsters. In St Albans – down Sandpit Lane. You used to beat me up! You used to beat me up every Thursday, when I was coming home from piano lessons.'

'But I didn't! Good Lord, Fizzell – it wasn't me!'

'You did! It was you! Wilkes was the name – Walloper Wilkes they used to call you. . .'

'Walloper Wilkes? No, no – that wasn't me, that was my cousin George. . .'

'Don't tell me that! Your mother lives in St Albans, doesn't she?'

'Yes, but. . .'

'So it *was* you! My mother lives in St Albans too, and she told me that when Walloper Wilkes grew up, he was a Pharmacist.'

'So – there you are! I've *never* been a Pharmacist.'

'Yes you have! Don't pretend that you haven't. The Gram Tam told me, ages ago. He told me what you put on your application form – a Supersonic Party-Political Pharmacist. Very cocky, I thought!'

'A what!' Mr Wilkes was laughing so hard, he had to lean against the door. 'A Supersonic Party-Political Pharmacist?' he gasped. 'Sorry – but that's just the Gram Tam again. . . . He's got it all wrong as usual! I didn't say *that*!'

'What did you say, then?'

'Sub-atomic Particle Physicist! It's completely different, you know.'

Fizzell stared suspiciously.

Mr Wilkes took a deep breath, and explained: 'Cousin George used to bully me, too. When *he* grew up he became a chemist – only he got too posh for that, and called himself a Pharmacist.'

'So it wasn't you?' frowned Fizzell.

'No. No – Scout's Honour!'

So they took the plunge, shook hands, and made it up.

'I tell you what,' said Mr Wilkes, 'I'll stand up for you at the trial.'

'It won't do any good,' said Fizzell gloomily.

'I don't know.' The Wizard looked thoughtful. 'It might.'

10

The saving of Fizzell's left ear

On the morning of the trial, the Gram Tam looked out of the window. 'Raining,' he announced. 'Coming down in stair-rods. D'you think it'll be rained off, this trial?'

The Gram Duchess told him not to be silly and to get ready quickly. He did; she inspected him; he passed, and they proceeded next door.

The trial was to be held in the Cinema. This may seem a trifle odd, but it was the only place that was suitable. The old Law Courts had been demolished years ago to make room for a motorway. The Magistrates' Courts were not big enough for everybody who wanted to come, and the Town Hall was in the middle of having its ceiling painted. So the Cinema it had to be.

It had been dressed for the occasion, of course. The Judge's Bench, the Witness Box, the Dock, had all been brought out of the lock-up garage where they'd lived a retired life, muffled in blankets, since the demolition of their old home. Polished and set in place, they made the 'Court' look most impressive.

It was eleven o'clock. In came the members of the Jury, looking self-conscious. In came the lawyers, in their black beetle robes and dusty white wigs. In came Justice Willibald Hake, and sat above them all, with a little hammer on the desk before him, just as though he were about to sell them all off at auction.

120

And last, they brought in Secretary Fizzell. He looked scared to death.

And no wonder! The Counsel for the Prosecution proved him guilty in no time at all. In fact, he spoke so cleverly, he could prove him guilty two or three times in one sentence. And as if that were not enough, he had a whole queue of witnesses waiting to prove he was guilty all over again.

He had witnesses who remembered the Cinema when it was the Palace ballroom. He had witnesses who had watched Fizzell negotiating with the Cinema proprietor, and witnesses who remembered the signing of the rent agreement. He had witnesses who could testify that the Cinema was a place of entertainment – he even had witnesses to say they'd seen Fizzell himself watching a film there once. ('It was "The Sound of Music",' they said).

Whatever could the Counsel for the Defence say, after that?

She didn't say a great deal, actually. She just asked the witnesses a few questions they weren't expecting. How did they know, she asked them, that the Palace and the ballroom were ever the same building? Well, they said, it was obvious: they were joined together. But, she asked, how did they *know* that they were joined together? Well, they said, you couldn't see a gap. How, she asked, would you know there was a gap if you saw it? They explained patiently, (thinking what a poor dumb barrister she was) that if there was a gap, you'd see the light between them.

'So,' she said, 'you would say that, if light can pass between two buildings, they cannot be joined together?'

'Suppose so,' they said.

'Thank you very much indeed,' she said, and smiled as sweetly as a spider smiles at a little fly in her web. 'Now, m'Lud,' she said to the Judge (who never seemed to mind being called such a silly name), 'I'd like to call a witness of my own. An expert witness – Mr Wilkes the Wizard.'

So up came Mr Wilkes, in his best robe, with his beard all brushed neatly. He put his hand on the big black Bible, and promised to tell the truth, the whole truth, and no fibs.

'Now, Mr Wilkes,' said the Counsel for the Defence, 'would you say that light can pass between these two buildings – the Palace and the Cinema?'

'Oh, yes,' said Mr Wilkes. 'I know it can. I'll show you if you like.'

'Good Heavens!' said the Judge, perking up. 'Can you really?'

'Certainly, m'Lud.' Mr Wilkes stepped down from the witness box, and walked out of the Court into the drizzling rain. Behind him scuttled the Judge, who beckoned the lawyers, the clerks, the jurors, and everyone else to follow. Out they all trooped, in a damp procession, round the back of the building, past the dustbins, to cluster round the downpipe from the gutter. There Mr Wilkes was making tiny adjustments to a tripod, upon which he had set up a curious piece of apparatus.

'Nothing magical, m'Lud,' he explained to the Judge, who was peering suspiciously at it through his other spectacles. 'Just an ordinary laser. Readily available; comes in kit form from the Open University. . .'

'Yes, yes,' said Justice Hake. 'Show the Court
how it works.'

So Mr Wilkes showed them how the laser could
shine a light on the cement-works chimney, half a
mile away.

'I say, what fun!' said the Judge. 'Can I have a
go?'

With the Wizard guiding his elbow (to prevent
judicial accidents, the laser being a dangerous
beast) he swung it round merrily. To the astonishment of all the shoppers, a disc of light scribbled
high across the back wall of Sparks and Spenders. It
came to rest over the Men's Underwear counter;
the Store Departmental Manager thought he'd seen
a vision, and was immediately converted to the
Plymouth Brethren.

It was judicially pronounced enormous fun.
When everybody had had a turn, Mr Wilkes shone

the laser straight at the wall in front of them, where the Cinema joined the Palace. (OR DID IT?)

'Now,' he said, 'Follow me.' And like a pantomime Pied Piper he led his motley troupe of gowns, wigs and curious faces round the front of the building. Standing by the downpipe, he held up a piece of paper, as though he were showing it to the wall. 'There you are!' he said.

And there was the light! It was shining right through the building, from back to front, to fall with a small burst of brilliance on the paper.

'It appears,' said Justice Willibald Hake, 'That there is indeed a gap!' He raised his eyebrows at the jury, in a meaningful sort of way.

They took the hint. And that was how it was that Secretary Fizzell was found Not Guilty.

After the trial, the Cinema manager had the decorators in, to spruce the old place up again. They found, oddly enough, two tiny holes drilled right through the walls, one at the front of the building, one at the back. They were dead level with one another. However, the decorators didn't think them worth mentioning, and filled them up with Polyfilla.

'*Absolutely* not.' The Duchess had made up her mind, and nothing would budge it. 'I never want to hear the name of Fizzell again! He's a traitor! A snake in the grass.'

'A traitor, you know,' nodded the Gram Tam, in case people hadn't got the point. 'A greek in, er . . . a sneak in the, um. . . We're not having him back, you know.'

'He's lucky to be acquitted,' said the Duchess. 'If I had my way, he'd be in prison for stealing the laws. No he can *not* have his job back!'

So that was that. Fizzell was Secretary no longer. He was out on his recently-rescued ear.

For a little while, this looked like a thoroughly good idea. Who needed a mean, devious, penny-pinching smarty-pants like Fizzell anyway? It was after a few Fizzell-less weeks that doubts began to creep in.

They crept, for instance, into the Public Transport people. They'd had a memo from the Gram Tam, something about their 'next ears bugit', with a lot of figures that didn't add up, and they couldn't make head nor tail of it. Then there was the Mayor, who was quite worried about 'putting on magic shoes in the Town Horl.' Where was he to get magic shoes in this day and age?

No sooner had P.M. de-mystified the Mayor ('Magic *shows*,' she suggested. 'Nothing to do with footwear.'), and sorted out the muddle of the Transport budget, than the Water Board were on the phone. What the blazes, they wanted to know, were they supposed to do with a 'sawn wood lock' on the reservoir?

P.M. suggested they bring the Gram Tam's note round right away. She polished her glasses carefully, and took a mouthful of gin. 'Now,' she said, 'let's have a look.'

The handwriting slopped back and forth across the page splattering bits of punctuation here and there at random. But the gist of it was – the Gram Tam thought '. . . a nenchanted sawn wood lock nice on the resofwar.' A what? A nenchanted sawn wood lock. . . Even P.M. was flummoxed. She read it out loud, tried it in various voices, without spectacles, with half-closed eyes. . .

'Ah!' She'd got it. 'A *swan*! An enchanted swan *would* look nice. . .' And, with a great weight removed from their minds, the Water Board went home.

But that wasn't the end of the problem! The Gram Tam's drivel started turning up everywhere; P.M. was snowed under, the Wizard was snowed under; nobody knew what they were supposed to be doing; government creaked to a halt. At last people could stand it no longer. An anxious deputation arrived at the Palace and asked to see the Duchess.

'For pity's sake, ma'am,' they said, 'bring back Secretary Fizzell! He may be a thief, and a sneak, and a cheat, and a liar, and a pain in the neck, and a mean old cheese-paring skinflint – but he can understand the Gram Tam's writing!! Bring him back,' they pleaded.

'Certainly not!' replied the Gram Duchess. 'After working for the SPAM, behind my back! I shall *never* forgive him.'

'But ma'am, His Exigency's messages – they're pure gibberish!'

'Then I shall send His Exigency to remedial spelling lessons.'

And she did. She arranged for the Gram Tam to have an hour's spelling lesson every morning, starting on the Monday. His teacher was to be Mrs Wright, a fine, large spelling teacher of twenty years' standing. ('Hm,' said the Gram Tam, 'I bet she sat down *sometimes*.')

Mrs Wright arrived at the first lesson with an

armful of books and an efficient smile. 'Now, sire,' she said brightly, 'we shall have you spelling beautifully in no time at all.'

'Oh, er – I can spell "beautifully". It's the other words I'm not so hot on.'

By the end of the week, things had changed enormously. You could see the difference at once. The Gram Tam's spelling was just as bad as ever, but Mrs Wright was a nervous wreck. Pale and trembling, she tapped on the Gram Duchess's door.

'I can't go on,' she quavered. 'It's hopeless, ma'am.'

'Why? Whatever is the matter?'

'His Exigency – he's got me so confused – I've forgotten how to *spell*! This morning, I left the "k" out of "wrong". . .'

And poor Mrs Wright fled the Palace, never to return.

After that, P.M. and the Wizard went to see the Duchess for one last try.

'Things are getting desperate, ma'am,' they said.

'What with the SPAM and the trial, and the spare bedroom, we're all behind with the magification!' said the Wizard.

'The paperwork in my office is four feet deep,' said P.M. 'And I'm only four feet six!'

'We're working like lunatics. . .'

'It's driving us bananas. . .'

'And if the Gram Tam goes on sending out memos of his own, there's going to be a catastrophe!'

'What exactly do you suggest?' asked the Duchess.

'Bring back Fizzell, ma'am,' they pleaded. 'He's

127

really sorry for what he did – he's *promised* to reform. And he used to do all this mountain of boring old paperwork, and the finance, and the economic thingies – and *he* understands the Gram Tam's writing!'

'Well. . .' said the Duchess.

They watched anxiously as the Duchess's mouth set itself into a thin straight line. She was thinking. . . Was she wavering? Would she say yes?

'I'll consider it,' she said. 'And I'll inform the Gram Tam what he has decided tomorrow morning.'

The next morning, however, before the Gram Tam could be issued with his decision, he got a letter. It had come airmail from the U.S.A.; 'Houston, Texas', said the postmark. The Gram Tam flipped it over as he munched his bacon and fried bread.

'Texas,' he munched, thoughtfully. 'Who do I know in Texas – mm? AH! Chickenwhatsit! It's old Chickenwhatsit at last – Muriel! Muriel, it's. . .'

'Yes, Percival,' said the Duchess. 'No doubt it's from Mr Schickenburger. Don't talk with your mouth full. It's rude.'

His mouth still full of bacon, the Gram Tam was already tearing open the envelope and pulling out the flimsy airmail paper. He put on a frown and his glasses, and stared at it a minute or two.

'No good,' he said at last. 'Can't make out a word of it. All in Chinese. Ah – no, er . . . here's a word. YAM. What's YAM?'

The Duchess took the letter, looked at it, and sighed heavily. 'You have it *back* to *front*.'

'What? – er. . .'

'You're looking at the back! The writing shows through this thin paper – turn it over! There. . .'

'Oh! Oh, er, yes, yes, yes. Not YAM – MAY! Ha – ha! May. May 1st – he's bringing seventy-two top businessmen to look at the Land of Magic on May 1st. . . Er, can we do it by then?'

11

And a good riddance to bad rubbish!

Christmas had come and gone; everybody was back at work. On an icy cold morning, with a vicious wind hurtling straight down from the North Pole, the Gram Tam and the Duchess ordered the chauffeur to bring out the Rolls. They were going on a tour of Diddlesdorf, to see how the Land of Magic was coming on.

'Well, what d'you think?' asked the Gram Tam cheerfully, as they passed the lemonade fountain, now frozen solid. An ogre was gloomily bashing a hole in the ice with his club, for the ducks. 'Not bad, eh?'

The Duchess, however, was not at all impressed. 'It won't do, Percival. It will not *do*.'

I have to admit, you could see her point. After all, you expect a Land of Magic to look a bit – well, magical, romantic, and so forth.

You don't expect to see a knight in shining armour wearing peacock-blue specs and cramming a personal stereo to his ear. You don't expect a magic Castlette with half a dozen petrol pumps and a car-wash in the forecourt. I suppose you could understand the damsels-in-distress wearing fur coats over their distressed-damsel dresses, what with the weather. But centrally-heated Olde Worlde Shopping Precincts, with plastic gnomes among the potted cheese-plants? Selling hi-fi and videos? Or Magic Grotto markets with '10p off Fish

Fingers' splashed across the window? And what about the band of magic Elf-Minstrels at the Bus Station, bashing out UB40's latest hit single with the help of a 500 watt amplifier?

'No,' said the Duchess, 'it doesn't have a magic *ring* to it at all!'

'Magic ring!' muttered the Gram Tam thoughtfully. 'Wonder if old Wilkes would make a. . .'

No, the Land of Magic hadn't got its act together at all. It looked half-baked, half-hearted – like the morning after the fancy-dress party and half the country hadn't got changed yet.

'I shall give the MOB a pep-talk!' said the Duchess.

'She's going to give you a proper talking-to!' the Gram Tam warned the MOB.

'There must be *drastic* changes!' declared the Duchess, when she had them all together and shut in. 'Drastic changes – and lots of hard work! We've wasted *months* of precious time with squabbles, and trials, and proclamations. Now we must *act*!'

'Er . . . I'm not much good at acting,' confessed the Gram Tam. 'I can do the pantomime horse – you know, the, er, rear end. . .'

The Duchess ignored him, and went on with her speech. 'Now, we've made a good start. The children of Diddlesdorf are really pulling their weight. But some of the grown-ups – and they know who they are! – will have to pull their socks up.

'If we're to have a Land of Magic by May 1st, we must all put our backs into it. And when I say all, I mean *all*. And that includes the Sensible People, and Secretary Fizzell, and the Duke of Potshotts, and everybody. We must bury the hatchet, put our shoulders to the wheel, our noses to the grindstone, and all pull together!'

'Er . . . er. . .' The Gram Tam, in an effort to be helpful, was busily scribbling notes. 'Er, what came after, um, "bury the ratchet"?'

So, in the end, the Duchess had agreed that Fizzell should have his old job back. He started work again that very afternoon.

He was a changed man. He *looked* much the same, to the naked eye – very like a plate of blancmange, really, if you dressed it up in a shirt and tie. But, as they say, the proof of the pudding. . .

Where he used to despise magic, Fizzell now worked day and night for the magification. Where he used to pour scorn on the MOB, now he joined it himself. And where he used to do everything he could to hinder the Wizard, now he made enormous efforts to help him. It was Fizzell who set up the 'Wizard's Department', and arranged for all sorts of experts – engineers, mechanics, electricians – to work for him. And he made sure they were all paid on time! Admittedly it still gave him indigestion to think how much it cost. But he sucked hard on his indigestion tablets, and tried not to think about it.

He made peace with the Duke of Potshotts too. He gave the Duke a written promise that he would never again try to make a rubbish dump, or anything else, on his safari park. And he sent his lion a late Christmas present, as a friendly gesture. (It was a woolly scarf. The lion ate it all up, but didn't think a lot of it.)

And the Sensible People? Oh, they were as bad

as ever. They went around like a bunch of wet Sundays, prophesying economic doom and financial ruin to all and sundry. 'Magic Costs Money' posters were suffocating half the trees in Diddlesdorf. You couldn't park your car for two minutes without a SPAM sticker appearing on the windscreen; even the pram wasn't safe from SPAM propaganda, and if the baby yelled, it got a SPAM lolly shoved in its mouth.

'Where do they get the money?' asked General Storr in astonishment.

'Must be subsidised by the Russians,' said Viscount Lobe.

The last straw came when the SPAM appeared on the television, on a Party Political Broadcast. 'Oh, no!' said the nation. 'Just as we were going to watch David Attenborough and the polar bears!' It was *so* tedious. They droned on and on about sensible policies and economic collapse until the whole of Diddlesdorf took refuge in a pot of tea.

The MOB felt it was time to retaliate. They would send their ultimate weapon, right into the SPAM's own camp.

And what was the weapon? Secretary Fizzell! It was P.M.'s idea. Fizzell could tell them why he'd changed *his* mind, she said, and persuade them to change *theirs*. If that didn't convert them, nothing would.

The negotiations started with the same old arguments for and against the magification. Finally, Fizzell said, 'Look, this is hopeless. When Mr Schickenburger comes with all his businessmen, we really cannot have a crowd of long-faced sensible protestors handing out anti-magic leaflets. It spoils the effect. Let's do a deal.'

'All right,' they said. 'What's it worth?'

'What do you want?'

'We want better parking facilities, a solution to the traffic problem, and a new Municipal Rubbish Tip. Fast!'

'Supposing we manage that?'

'You get our full co-operation with the magic scheme.'

'And supposing we don't?'

'You get false noses.'

Fizzell wasn't sure he'd heard properly. 'You . . . you what?'

'We'll all go around wearing big red false noses. We'll have them on when Schickenburger and his crowd come. Then we'll put a rumour about that anybody who stays in Diddlesdorf gets a revolting swollen nose.'

'Well, you rotten swine! What a nasty trick!'

'It is, isn't it?' they said. 'You won't get a single tourist anywhere *near* the place.'

Meanwhile, back at the Palace, the MOB had come to a decision. We can't possibly get everything finished by May 1st, they said. So we'll have to concentrate on one *big* thing. Something to impress Mr Chickenwhatsit and all his merry admen.

'Exactly! Exactly!' cried the Gram Tam. 'Just what I, er. . . A Dragon! That's what we need – a nice, big, fiery, ferocious Dragon. . .'

At which point Fizzell came in to report what he had agreed with the SPAM.

'A new Rubbish Tip,' groaned the Wizard. 'I *knew* it. When?'

'By May 1st'.

So there it was. The whole situation was perfectly clear – and utterly impossible. Mr Wilkes was in a quandary.

'A Dragon,' said the MOB. 'By May 1st.'

'A Rubbish Tip,' said the SPAM. 'By May 1st.'

'Never mind about the Tip,' said the MOB. 'It's the *Dragon* that's important.'

'Forget the Dragon,' said the SPAM. 'It's the *Tip* that's essential.'

'If we don't get the Dragon,' nagged the MOB, 'all the money we paid to Mr Schickenburger's wasted. We'll *never* be a proper Land of Magic. . .'

'If we don't get that Rubbish Tip,' threatened the SPAM, 'you won't see a tourist within fifty miles of Diddlesdorf – ever again!'

'So you bear that in mind!'

'So you just think about it!'

One bright, sparkling, snowy morning, Mr Wilkes gave up. He'd thought, and thought, and thought – and still his brain was as empty as a beach hut in January. 'I can't do this,' he thought. 'I'm beaten. I'll resign. I'll go and live in Luton – and work for the Gas Board. Or something.'

'I'm no good!' he yelled at the computer. 'I'm a FAILURE!' And he tore off his Wizard's Robe, pulled on his parka, and went for a walk. 'Might as well see the sights,' he said to himself, 'before I leave Diddlesdorf for good.'

So he trudged up the mountain, and wandered round the Devil's Kitchen, that curious chasm that the Gram Tam used to go on about.

It's funny how these things happen. To the

astonishment of a few sheep, Mr Wilkes suddenly let out a great yell. Then he leapt away down the mountain, arms waving above his head, like somebody conducting the 1812 Overture while running the forty metres.

'Got it!' he gasped, breathless, round Peony Moondrop's door. 'I've got an IDEA!' And off he whirled again to start work.

There wasn't a moment to lose. The Wizard's Department went into action at once. The MOB was mobilized. The Gas Board was forgotten. There were comings and goings of labourers and lorry-drivers, accountants and aviation experts, miners and marketing men, civil servants and civil engineers. It was all right so long as you didn't mix them up. The accountants didn't like being offered regulation hard helmets, and the miners got worried when offered a balance sheet to work on.

The Gram Tam tried his best, but was discovered in a state of shock one day after accidentally offering a mug of tea with two sugars to a senior civil servant. Eventually the Gram Duchess made everybody wear large labels to say what job they were doing. After that it was all much more straightforward. In fact, labels became quite fashionable in Diddlesdorf. P.M. had one saying 'Prime Minister', and the Gram Tam had one that read 'Gram Tam'.

Thus labelled, they buzzed back and forth, day after day. Up the mountain and down the mountain they scurried, between the Wizard's Headquarters and the big Secret.

And *what* a Secret! You couldn't get *near* the thing. All the paths of the mountain were closed. The Secret itself was shrouded in a huge sort of tent, of scaffolding and tarpaulins. No one could get in without a pass, and anyone found snooping round about was shooed away.

But what about the people working on it? *They* must know what it was. Reporters ambushed them as they hurried to and fro. 'What is it?' they asked.

'*We* don't know,' said the workers.

'But you *must* do!'

'No we don't. We just do what the Wizard says. We won't know what it is till it's all put together.'

Rumours buzzed about, thick as midges on a summer day. It was a Dragon. It wasn't a Dragon. It was a Rubbish Tip. It wasn't a Rubbish Tip. It wasn't a Dragon or a Rubbish Tip: it was a remote-controlled mushroom farm, or a space-rocket launching pad, or a gigantic plastic chicken-and-hamburger. . .

'Hope it's a Dragon!' yelled the children.

'It had better *not* be a Dragon!' growled the Sensible People.

Spring came, and the snow melted. The Secret stayed – Secret. People were spying and prying, and ferreting and fishing, but nobody knew what it was. Then one morning towards the end of April, the word went out – 'They're taking the covers off!'

And so they were: workmen were taking down the tarpaulins, dismantling the scaffolding. What would it be? What would it be? A huge crowd gathered round, breathless, to watch. . . And there it was!

Nothing at all.

A fence round some mud, and trampled grass, gone yellow where the tent had covered it.

'What *is* it?' they demanded of the Wizard,

137

whenever he set foot outside his house.

'You'll see,' he said. 'On May 1st.'

At last Mayday itself dawned, grey and damp and drizzly. Mr Schickenburger emerged from his aeroplane with all his seventy-two followers behind him. They were advertising people, photographers, tour operators, travel agents, airline executives – anybody who might make money out of Mr Schickenburger's holiday paradise. Would it really be a Land of Magic?

'Isn't it FABULOUS!' cried Mr Schickenburger to anybody he could reach, and slapped them on the back in case they'd dozed off. 'Isn't this just a *phee*-nomenal Land of Magic? Look at that!!' he enthused, and 'Look at this!', and 'What's *that*?'

'Um, oh!' said the Wizard, nervously, 'That's a . . . magic telephone booth, yes, and that's a . . . magic hot-dog stall.'

'And what's that?' Mr Schickenburger pointed at a typical tatty Diddlesdorf Portakabin – the one that housed the Housing Department.

'Oh, er. . ' – Mr Wilkes was sweating under his robe – 'That, er . . . that's a woodcutter's hut! Magic woodcutter's hut. . .'

'Is that *right*?' exclaimed Mr Schickenburger. 'And what's that?' He peered up into the sky and pointed.

They all squinted up into the brightening sky. Everyone could hear what he meant – it was like somebody next door doing the hoovering – but no one could see it. . .

And suddenly, above the rooftops – there it was!
A DRAGON!

138

A gigantic Dragon, red and green and gold – it was sailing sedately on outstretched filmy wings just above the chimney-pots. It was *magnificent*. So close it flew, you could see its tongue flickering! So close, that you could see the men in its cabin. . .

Yes, it was the most breath-taking Dragon-airship you'll ever see.

The huge beast hovered and came in to land, first on the Senior School playing field. People ran in from all sides, swarming round for a glimpse of the wonder.

'Hm!' snorted the Sensible People. 'A dragon – is that all? If that Wizard hasn't made a new Rubbish Tip, there'll be. . .'

'RUBBISH!' roared the Dragon, in a great loudspeaker boom. Everybody jumped.

'Rubbish!' the Dragon boomed again. 'House-hold rubbish, garden rubbish – feed me your rubbish! I'm a Rubbish-Eating Dragon!'

'Wow-ee!!' yelled Mr Schickenburger. 'Did you hear *that*? Did you hear *that*?'

And while Mr Schickenburger slapped some backs, the Dragon opened her doors to receive the rubbish. At last, she spoke again. She invited them all to come to see herself and her mate, at the Dragons' Lair, at three o'clock. Then she explained how to get there.

Finally, with a wave of her wings, she lifted herself from the ground, and flew off to beg rubbish somewhere else.

There's a well-known saying, 'You don't refuse an offer from a Dragon' – or at any rate, there ought to be. Nobody refused this Dragon's invitation. From all over Diddlesdorf they came, some walking, most by Hoverrug. An endless furry caterpillar of Hoverrugs wriggled up the mountain, up and up, as the weather cleared and the sun came out. They stopped at the place that used to be called the Devil's Kitchen – and was now the Dragon's Lair.

Mr Schickenburger and his supporters were put on a special platform (in case they got in the way). It overlooked a little rocky valley, that slid down the mountainside and flattened to nothing among the trees below. Underneath was a crack in the ground. Just a crack, mostly not more than a few inches wide; but at the lower end, the Wizard's Engineers had forced the crack open with explosives. . . And there, down there below, was a vast, vast cave! You could have put Wembley Stadium down there, and still have had room for the Houses of Parliament. With its massive squat pillars of stone, it was a home fit for giants – or Dragons.

And there he was: the big one! Look – down there, behind those ugly pillars of rock! A glint of a cold eye, and the long, long jaws, still as stone. He must be a mile long!

People were jostling; cameras were clicking. Mr Schickenburger and the Gram Tam were shaking hands, and slapping backs, and congratulating one another, and shaking hands again, and slapping backs again, until the Duchess told the Gram Tam to stop it at once or he'd be sick.

Further up the valley, the crack had been widened to a gaping hole. By it rested the flying airship Dragon, inside a fenced paddock of her own. All day she had worked, bringing monstrous stacks of rubbish from Diddlesdorf's collapsed Tip. Now she was sending it, clattering and swooshing, down the chute into the Dragon's Lair beneath. There it settled, a giant pile in a still more giant space.

Three o'clock. Time for the Gram Tam's speech. He did it beautifully. The Duchess had written it all out and tied it to his sleeve with a piece of elastic, so that he couldn't mislay it. He said it all clearly; didn't lose his place, or get it in the wrong order. It was perfect – except that nobody heard a word of it. The microphone wasn't on.

What happened next, not everybody could see. But those who did see never forgot it. The Gram Tam, at a nod from the Wizard, pulled on a special cord. . .

And down in the Lair, the Dragon moved forward. The crowd held its breath. The great jaws opened, *so* slowly. You could see the teeth! You could see the shining tongue! Then, a deafening roar of fiery breath, and the whole mighty heap of

rubbish in the lair was shooting flames. Fierce
bouncing flames, they were cracking and spitting
and thrusting – and the whole heap, melting into
one fiery globe, was sinking, and gradually sinking, and falling back, slowly, to a tame heap of ash.

A stunning show! No one could take their eyes
off it. Especially the Gram Tam, who seemed not to
be taking his eyes off it for an awfully long time. . .

What *is* he doing? Why's he holding on to that
cord with one hand and flapping like that with the
other?

Suddenly the loudspeakers were on, and the
Gram Tam's voice booming through them:

'Wilkes! Wilkes! I've done it *again*!'

'What, sire?'

'Got me blasted *fingers* caught in the thingy. . .'